MARY

S S SAYWACK

A MARY FINCH MYSTERY

MARY Finch

and the

THIEF

S S Saywack

Cover design and formatting S S Saywack
All enquiries to: saywackwrites@gmail.com
First published 2021
Print ISBN: 978-1-8383904-0-2
eISBN: 978-1-8383904-1-9

For Aria and Luna.

Sorry, no dragons, princesses or fairies.

But there is a cat!

I

LADY MARY FINCH

'Finch! Are you slacking again?' The gravelly voice coming from the bottom of the stairwell caused Mary to drop the penny dreadful she was reading.

'No, Mr Boots. Coming, Mr Boots,' Mary shouted back, hurrying downstairs.

'Get your shawl on,' the butler said. 'Miss Leticia wants a quarter of pear drops, Miss Portia, sherbet lemons, and Miss Rosamund, marshmallows. Come on, chop-chop, girl.'

'But Mr Boots, it's gone eight. Mr Marshall's will be closed.'

'I can tell the time perfectly well, Finch. Now get off with you, girl.'

Mary trudged back to her room, found her threadbare shawl and pulled it tightly across her head and shoulders.

It wasn't enough she had her usual chores to do: all the scrubbing of the tables and floors, the washing of pots and pans and sheets, blacking the cooking range (which she hated), bringing coal up from the coal cellar, but she also had to cater to the whims of her employer's daughters.

She hated being *just* a scullery maid as much as she hated blacking the cooking range. As positions in households go, it was the lowest of the low. But as she always said, that meant there was only one direction she could go, and that was up. And Mary had plans.

Even so, as she glanced out of her attic window into the darkness, she sighed. It had been snowing all day. Everywhere was white – the streets, the gardens, the roofs. Even the Lions of Trafalgar Square, she knew, would be wearing white capes and Nelson a white hat. She saw her reflection – a girl with gentle grey eyes and straight mousey brown hair gazed solemnly back at her. A hungry girl, who had not yet had her dinner.

She felt miserable.

'It's not fair,' she complained to the cat, Oscar, who looked up from the bed, yawned and gave her a *well, you are the scullery maid, after all* look.

'At least you've got a fur coat,' Mary said, 'and all the scraps from the kitchen you can eat, and a nice place to sleep.'

Oscar yawned again, not the least bit interested.

As Mary left the house, her best friend, Emma the chambermaid, gave her a sympathetic look. Their employer, Mr Grimwig, and his family were meant to be out tonight, but the foul weather had persuaded them to stay indoors. The triplets were bored – and when they were bored, they ate. And they were often bored.

Mr Marshall, Confectioner to the Elite, had a shop just off Oxford Street. It was a full mile and then some from the Grimwigs' house on Regent's Park. Bending her head against the wind as the snow flurried past, Mary hurried down Baker Street, past Sherlock Holmes's flat, past her friend Archie's shop, and into Oxford Street, her feet crunching into fresh, crispy snow, grumbling to herself as she rushed along. The triplets were the most spoilt brats she knew. Sweets at this time of night, as if there wasn't anything else in the pantry they could eat. Spoilt was too nice a word for them – she could quite easily think of others.

To her surprise, Oxford Street was busy and a few shops were still open. But when she reached Mr Marshall's, it was just as she knew it would be: closed. She dared not go back empty-handed, which only left one option: knocking. She did so, loudly. Not once, but three times, until a window opened on the first floor. A lump of snow, dislodged from the sill, fell and narrowly missed her.

An angry voice boomed from above.

'We're closed! What does the sign say? Doesn't it say closed? Isn't that what it says? Closed? Or can't you read? Closed!'

Mary ambled into the middle of the street and gazed up into the dark, scowling face of Mr Marshall, who was leaning out of the window. A napkin was around his neck and a fork with a speared roast potato in his hand.

'I can read very well, thank you,' Mary said.

'Then you must be daft if you don't know what it means.'

'I do know what it means, and I ain't daft.'

'Simple then.'

'Simple neither,' Mary huffed.

'Get off home, or I'll call a bluebottle, you dull-witted girl.'

Mary choked back her anger. In her most polite voice and with a smile, she said, 'I want some pear drops, sherbet lemons and marshmallows, please.'

'You want? You want? We're closed. That means shut. Not open. Read the sign. Come back tomorrow.'

It was no use – Mary knew it had to be done. She stood with her hands on her hips and fixed an adamant stare on to the sweet-shop owner. Taking a deep breath, she bellowed so everyone around could hear.

'Well, you see, Mr Marshall, it's like this. Either you're open, or you're not, in which case I'll take my business to Mr Jones's shop up the road – *my* business, of course, being Mr Grimwig's business, and it's *his* business that brings me here.'

The scowl immediately left Mr Marshall's face. Taking advantage of his stunned silence, Mary roared, 'Miss Leticia *Grimwig* wants pear drops, Miss Portia *Grimwig* wants sherbet lemons and Miss Rosamund *Grimwig* wants marshmallows!'

Mr Marshall brightened. A smile appeared on his face and his eyes opened widely. It was as if his head was a lamp and someone had suddenly turned it on.

'Well, why didn't you say so in the first place? Of course, we're open. Look at the time – it's still early. It's not even nine yet. Be right down. Don't go away. One minute, please.'

Moments later, the bolts of the shop were drawn back and the door opened. The rotund frame of Mr Marshall, shrouded in a richly patterned dressing gown, the napkin still tucked into the front of his shirt, filled the doorway.

'And how's the master?' His fawning voice matched his fawning smile. There was a twinkle in his eyes. 'Does *he* want anything? And I've got the mistress's favourite – some lovely boiled sweets. Just in, they are. She'd love them, she would.'

Mary sighed. It was always the same. Mention the name Grimwig and everyone suddenly became available. And why not? They were as rich as kings. They owned a big house on Regent's Park. They owned a cotton mill in

Lancashire. And to think that ten or so years ago, they and several others had lived in a two-up-two-down in Manchester with barely tuppence to rub together. Now look at them! How could they have got so wealthy, so quickly?

Like a spectre, Mrs Marshall, a thin, pasty-faced woman, haunted the counter. She wiggled and jiggled, delighted to be of service to such eminent patrons.

'Oh! How good of you to come all this way at this hour in such atrocious weather, and just for the girls!' she gushed as she watched her husband dole out the sweets. 'Only the best for the girls, only the very best, Mr Marshall.'

'Of course, my dear, of course.'

'And put in an extra one,' she whispered to her husband and smiled at Mary.

Mr Marshall winked. 'And one more for Miss Portia, I think,' he said and they both tittered. Mary drummed her fingers restlessly. She was anxious to be away and home.

Before long, three parcels rested on the counter, each neatly secured with a scarlet ribbon tied in a bow.

'There,' Mr Marshall said. 'Now you give the girls my very best wishes.'

'And tell them,' Mrs Marshall added, 'that Mr Marshall hopes they enjoy his most marvellous confectionery, and they should tell their friends about it.'

‘Of course, Mrs Marshall,’ Mary said with a sour smile, murmuring, ‘I’m sure they’ll listen to a fourteen-year-old scullery maid.’

‘Well, off you go. Don’t keep the girls waiting,’ Mr Marshall said sharply and gave her an annoyed glare. Clapping his hands, he shooed her out of his shop.

Mary started back the way she had come. She would have to hurry; she didn’t want to linger, not with Jack still about, and no one had caught him yet. What was the Ripper’s last count? Ten? Or was it eleven he’d murdered? She might be a long way from Whitechapel and he hadn’t been around for a few years, but you never know.

She rushed up Baker Street. When she got back, there would be the clearing up to do, and then the washing up before bed. In the morning, all the fires would need lighting, the laundry collecting, and that was just before breakfast. But first, she would have to listen to the Grimwig sisters arguing over which sweet was the best.

Mary shivered. It was less from the cold and more from the triplets’ voices that she could hear in her head – their penetrating nasal screeches, like fingernails dragged down a blackboard. She bent her head against the wind and forged along, imagining she was Lady Mary Finch, intrepid Arctic explorer, Queen Victoria’s trusted envoy of discovery.

With eyes screwed up tightly against the driving snow

and mouth set firm, Lady Mary Finch pressed on gamely through the pack ice...

By the time she rounded the corner into Regent's Park, she had worked up quite a sweat. However, as she had warmed up, her temper had cooled. Mary could see the house just ahead. In a few minutes, she would be home. In an hour, she would be in bed with all the chores completed. Oscar would be curled up beside her and she could finish reading the story in her latest penny dreadful magazine. She was halfway through *The Vampire's Curse* and wanted to know how it ended.

Lady Mary Finch had completed her voyage of discovery and was finally home. Just one more turn and she'd be through the gates of the palace, her precious treasures secure. Her Majesty Queen Victoria would be there to present her with the royal sash of distinction.

'It is with great pleasure that we honour the achievement of this remarkable young woman. Against insurmountable odds, she persevered to...'

Just as Mary turned into the entrance path, *finally home,* she collided with a stranger leaving the house. She was crouching low against the wind and he was hurrying (though hurtling might better describe his progress) so neither saw each other.

It was the most resounding crash.

2

A MEETING IN THE SNOW

To her horror, Mary saw her *precious treasures* scatter across the ground. It was all she could do to gather them whilst entangled with the stranger. Thankfully, the parcels were still securely tied.

Mary stuttered an apology. 'Sorry, mister, I weren't looking…'

The stranger said nothing.

'Here, ain't you…?' Mary had seen him before, but she stopped speaking when she noticed the front door was open. Footprints in the snow showed he'd come down the steps. The warm yellow light from the passageway pooled around them. She looked at his worn unpolished shoes, at his creased working clothes and the flat cap pulled across his head. He was no gentleman. He was definitely not someone who would leave the house by the front door.

'Oi! Why didn't you use the tradesman's entrance?' she asked, puzzled.

Their eyes met. His weathered face shone brightly with sweat, despite the icy air. His gaze, however, was a mask of anger as cold as the night. To Mary's surprise, he pushed her backwards.

'What're you doing?' Mary yelled.

The stranger was on his knees. His head snapped left and right, over his shoulders and back again. His darting eyes explored the ground. He reached out his hands and his fingers ferreted around and about through the snow, searching for something. When he could not find it, he cursed bitterly. Mary flinched as she saw him raise his arm. His fist was balled and she cowered in expectation of the blow she feared was about to fall on her.

Just then, a piercing scream erupted from within the house, followed by terrible screeches. He froze.

'Thief! Thief! Thief!' Mrs Grimwig shouted over and over, hardly stopping to draw breath.

The vaguely familiar stranger grimaced in horror, glared at Mary. His nostrils flared and his breast heaved as the ringing cries continued to fill his ears. Again his head snapped back to the open door. He could not conceal his panic.

'Get outta my way,' he shouted. He pushed Mary back and was off, racing away across the street.

Mary's terror had turned to anger. As she struggled to

get up, she gritted her teeth and scowled at the retreating figure. Mrs Grimwig's shouts told her all she needed to know.

'Oi! You! Stop!' Mary hollered. She chased after him, still clutching her parcels. In her hurry, she barely noticed the uproar behind her. Nor did she hear the shrill police whistle that the butler blew. Several sharp blasts cut through the heavy snow-filled air. She didn't hear the answering whistles coming from several directions; she was entirely focused on catching the thief.

'Oi, stop!' she bellowed again.

The thief was quick, far quicker than she, and he moved swiftly up the empty street. His tread was firm and confident while hers was slipping and sliding as she tried to keep up. He was fast disappearing into the gloom ahead. Mary struggled on, not yet ready to give up the chase. She stretched her legs and bent her head, determined to catch him, though what she'd do when she did, she had not considered.

'Gotcha!' someone shouted behind her and Mary's head jerked back. She screamed in pain; she was being pulled backwards. Her arms windmilled. Her feet slipped and slid. Yet again that night, she found herself on the ground.

A dark figure loomed over her. Mary could make out his heavy coat, his bright buttons and the tall hat perched on his head. His eyes fixed her with a cutting gaze. He still had hold of her hair, and as he slowly leant forward, a smile curled his lips.

'You ain't going nowhere,' he whispered and blew a hard, long blast on a whistle.

Several people, more police and Mr Boots converged, answering the call. Soon Mary was surrounded as they stood over her. She looked at each in turn, at their silent accusatory gazes: looks she did not care for one bit.

'I'm not the thief,' Mary shouted at the policeman holding her hair. 'Let me go, you daft twit.'

'Now, now, Miss. Name-calling? That's not very ladylike, is it?' he said sarcastically.

'He's getting away.' She motioned angrily up the street. 'Don't just stand there, get after him.'

'Is that so, Miss?' the policeman said in a slow and deliberate manner. There was an air of triumph in his voice.

'Mr Boots,' Mary shouted to the butler, who now stood beside her, half bent with his hands on his knees, panting hard. 'Tell them to get after him… He's getting away–'

Mary was startled as the butler leant forward, his face dark with menace. She shied back and away, suddenly fearful.

'Shame on you, Finch!' Mr Boots scowled at her between breaths.

'What?'

'The Grimwigs trusted you, Mary Finch. They gave you a position and a home. This is how you repay them?'

'Mr Boots?' Mary said. She gawped as the butler came closer.

'Stealing from them? Biting the hand that fed you? Betraying their trust?'

'What, Mr Boots?' She looked at him, puzzled.

'It was Mr Grimwig's Christian charity what saved you from the streets, Finch. I was going to say saved you from a life of crime – hah!' He spat the words at her and Mary scrambled back some more until she was resting against the policeman's legs behind her and could go no further. 'You were a wrong 'un and I told him as much the day he hired you. You're too shifty, Finch, by far. No, he said, she deserves a chance. Mark my words, I said, the first chance she gets, she'll rob you blind. What a shame I was right and that good man was wrong. *What a shame,* Finch.'

Mary sat, stunned. She seethed at Mr Boots in both astonishment and anger, unable to believe what she was hearing.

'What are you on about, Mr Boots? Rob him? But I ain't never stole a thing in my life.' A round of laughter broke out. 'The thief, Mr Boots – he's getting away–' She flicked her head and pointed in the direction the stranger had gone.

'And what's this, then?' the policeman asked,

nodding to something on the ground beside her. 'I reckon we've got you bang to rights, young lady.'

Mary's mouth gaped wide. Along with the three parcels of sweets for the Grimwig children was a fourth package: a cloth bag. It was open. Spilling out were Mrs Grimwig's jewels. Lying in the snow were a diamond necklace and earrings, brooches and pins, several rings and chains and other gems. The diamonds glinted and sparkled brightly, even under the subdued light of the street lamp.

3

NOTHING IS MISSING

Mary was frog-marched, prodded and pushed all the way to the Grimwigs' house. Each of her protests was ignored. It was a firm shove from the policeman that eventually propelled Mary through the front door. She almost stumbled and fell.

The policeman, Constable O'Connor, had a triumphant look on his face, as opposed to the stern glare on Mr Boots's. O'Connor produced the stolen jewels with the flair of a magician performing a trick. His audience – Mr and Mrs Grimwig, their children, and a gathering of maids and footmen – gasped in horror.

'Caught her in the act, sir.' Constable O'Connor beamed. 'She tried to leg it, but she couldn't outrun me,' he said proudly, puffing out his chest with the satisfaction of a job well done.

'But I didn't steal nothing,' Mary implored. 'You ain't listening to me.'

'It's jail for you, girl. Here you are, Mr Grimwig,' and O'Connor handed the jewels over. 'I checked, sir. She's not got a thing else on her.'

Mr Grimwig sighed and shook his head. 'Well, I am disappointed,' he said.

'But I didn't steal them, sir,' Mary pleaded again. Her heart was pounding as she looked into Mr Grimwig's dark, impassive eyes. 'Honest, sir, I must have picked them up when I bumped into the thief who was leaving the house – he must have dropped them.'

'Likely story!' the policeman said. 'Your accomplice, was it?' He took out his notebook, licked the tip of his pencil and began writing.

'Mr Grimwig, sir, please, this is all a mistake,' Mary begged.

'The only mistake you made was getting caught.' Constable O'Connor gave a contemptuous laugh. 'They're all innocent, sir, even when we catch them red-handed.'

Mary glared at him. She looked to Mr Grimwig in the desperate hope that he would hear her out.

'I went chasing after the crook when I heard Mrs G shout thief–'

'Manners!' Mr Boots growled.

‘Sorry, Mr Grimwig. I meant when the *mistress* shouted thief.’

‘A likely story,’ Constable O’Connor said again with a tut. ‘More like you legged it because your plan didn’t work, and seeing everyone was chasing you, you thought you’d better get a move on yourself.’

‘What are you talking about?’ Mary said.

‘She probably did have an accomplice, sir,’ O’Connor explained. ‘Did the switch, or *tried* to – it’s an old trick. If he’s spotted and has to leg it, he passes her the loot, and she comes back inside the house with the gems hidden on her, acting all innocent and sweet, while we go on a wild goose chase after her partner. If we catch him, he’ll have nothing on him and we’ll look like fools. They were probably going to meet up later for shares. But when your good wife shouted thief, this one–’ he prodded Mary in the back, ‘–must have panicked.’

A scowl twisted Mary’s lips, both for the accusation and the push.

‘If you’d caught him, we could have settled this there and then,’ she said.

‘He was a bit quicker than you, wasn’t he?’ O’Connor raised his eyebrows. ‘Abandoned you, did he? He weren’t going to hang about, that’s for sure.’

‘He was leaving a trail as clear as anything in the snow – you didn’t need to be Rex the bleedin’ tracker dog to follow it,' Mary said angrily. 'His trail's probably all covered up by now!'

'And I don't need to be Mr *bleedin'* Sherlock Holmes to figure out your game!'

Mr Grimwig raised his hand for quiet. Immediately everyone fell silent.

There was an odd look in his eyes that made Mary fearful of the pronouncement she knew was coming. She wished he would let her speak. If he gave her a chance, she felt sure she could explain the misunderstanding. But each time she tried, O'Connor interrupted.

Mary swallowed dryly, bit her lip in frustration, took a deep breath and waited.

'Is it true?' Mr Grimwig said. 'The jewels were found beside you?'

Mary nodded.

'And another individual was involved?'

Again, she nodded.

'And you maintain you had nothing to do with the theft?'

She shook her head and silently mouthed, *nothing.*

'Yet you had the jewels!'

'But… the other gent–' Mary's anguished plea was stopped as Mr Grimwig's hand came up yet again. He emptied the remainder of the bag's contents onto a side table. The jewels clattered across the polished mahogany as he scanned them with a seemingly idle gaze. Having turned the bag inside out, he ran his fingers through his shining black hair. His forehead wrinkled for a moment as he chewed his bottom lip, then he looked at his wife who was leaning over the bannister. The two exchanged glances.

'And… this is all? There is… no more?' he said hesitantly.

He looked at the policeman, who first nodded, and then shook his head. Then Mr Grimwig looked at Mary and scrutinised her intently. She felt small under his gaze and looked away.

Mrs Grimwig, a pretty flaxen-haired woman with a heavily powdered face and rouged lips, clutched the bannister rail until her knuckles whitened. Mary watched with trepidation, as well as fascination, as various contortions twisted the woman's face – she had never seen the mistress like this before. A red wave rose from her neck to colour her cheeks and forehead, and her eyes narrowed and swivelled, fixing Mary with a furious glare.

'Where are they?' she screamed. 'Do you hear? Has your friend got them? You… you… you little thief–' and her lips trembled.

'Dora!' Mr Grimwig said firmly. 'We have company.' His penetrating stare stopped her with one foot hanging in mid-air. He nodded sharply towards the policeman.

Mrs Grimwig's eyes widened and slewed around and fell on to the puzzled face of Constable O'Connor.

'B-b-but these are them, aren't they?' the policeman stuttered, glancing at the Grimwigs, Mary and the gems in turn.

'Dora, we have the jewels back,' Mr Grimwig said in a firm, commanding voice.

The policeman licked the tip of his pencil again and carefully placed it on a page of his notebook, and it stayed there, unmoving. His baffled stare continued to shift between Mr and Mrs Grimwig, Mary and the jewels, and back to the notebook.

'See. They are *all* back,' Mr Grimwig said. '*Each* and every one. Dora, nothing is missing.'

Dora Grimwig's eyes widened. 'But Jim–'

'*Nothing* is missing,' James Grimwig repeated through tightly gritted teeth. 'Letty, collect Mama's jewels.' He handed the empty bag to his daughter and turned on his heels to face his wife, wiping away a trickle of sweat that ran down his cheek as a knot of muscle tightened at the corners of his jaws.

Leticia Grimwig swept the gems into the bag and paused only to snatch the three bags of sweets out of Mary's hand. She walked up the stairs, a scornful nose in the air. Both Portia and Rosamund, assuming a similar attitude of contempt, followed their sister until only the clicking of their heels on the parquet flooring could be heard along the upstairs corridor.

'I am truly disappointed with you, Mary,' Mr Grimwig said softly.

Mary's shoulders drooped. Her hopes were collapsing like a deflated balloon, because far from looking disappointed, he looked annoyed.

'Do you know this… this man you bumped into?' Mr Grimwig asked as he slowly turned to look at her, a grim smile tightening his lips. 'You mentioned another person leaving the house.'

Mary looked up, happy that she would get her chance to say what had happened.

'Sir–' As Mary began to speak, a sharp intake of breath came from her friend Emma, whose hands had shot up to her mouth. There was a look of horror on her face. And suddenly, Mary knew where she had seen the thief before.

She hesitated. In the heavy silence, time seemed to pass very slowly. It was definitely fear in her friend's eyes – of that she was certain.

'S-s-sir…' she garbled and her frightened gaze rose up to meet Mr Grimwig's.

'Well?' Mr Grimwig gave her an impatient stare.

'Come on, girl. Answer the gentleman,' Constable O'Connor said and, to hurry her along, nudged her once again in the back.

Mary broke out in a cold sweat. She glanced at her friend again. There was no doubt about it – Emma knew the thief. Slowly, her eyes crawled around to look at Mr Grimwig.

'S-s-sir…' she gulped and swallowed heavily.

Constable O'Connor, Mr and Mrs Grimwig and Mr Boots were all watching her. And so were Emma Watkins and the rest of the maids and footmen of the household. She could not feel more under a spotlight than she did now. She shrank before their gaze.

'N-No, sir, I-I…' Her voice, a barely audible mumble, sounded hollow, as if it had come up from a deep well, and the words hung limply in the air.

A darkness washed Mr Grimwig's face.

'So, let me get this right,' he said slowly. He came closer to tower over her and Mary shrank back even further as she looked up into his cold, hard eyes. 'There was another man. You don't know who he was, and yet you had my wife's jewels in your possession, which you maintain he stole.'

For a moment, Mary knew she could save herself – all she had to do was tell Mr Grimwig where she'd first seen the man. But if she did, it would land her friend in as much trouble as she herself was in right now. That was something she could not do. She shied away in embarrassment. Her face flushed scarlet and she felt decidedly ill. The very idea that her friend, the only real one she had in the household, would conspire to steal from the Grimwigs was absurd – Emma was far too honest.

She stared glumly at the floor.

'Right then,' Constable O'Connor said brightly, putting away his notebook with a flourish. 'Let's go, young lady – I've got a nice cell waiting for you.'

4
MR GRIMWIG DECIDES

'A moment of your time, Constable,' Mr Grimwig said.

How quickly he became calm. Coupled with his shrewd and calculating stare, this made Mary instantly nervous. It was enough that she was about to be arrested, but his sudden change of mood frightened her. She was fearful of what it all meant.

'Dora! Boots!' he called and walked briskly towards the drawing room. Dora Grimwig grimaced at Mary as she went past.

'Does no one have duties?' Mr Boots asked as he puffed out his chest and huffed at the audience of maids and footmen standing idly watching. 'Well? This is not a music hall and there will be no more gawping. Or do I have to find things for you to do?'

The maids and footmen turned to leave.

'And remember!' Mr Boots boomed after them. 'What goes on in this house, stays in this house. You had better believe that because if I hear one whisper of what happened tonight, one little story in a pub, I'll have the tattle-tale out on the street faster than you can say Jack Robinson.'

In an instant, the hallway cleared. With that, Mr Boots joined the Grimwigs in the drawing room, closing the door behind him and leaving Mary and the policeman alone.

Soon, raised voices could be heard from behind the door. There were shouts followed by moments of quiet, and then it would start all over again. The mistress hollered something. Urgent hushing noises followed.

As the argument rose and fell, Mary and O'Connor waited patiently. Now and then, the policeman's lips would curl into a happy grin, become serious again, before curling up once more. Each time he smiled, his eyes lit up. Mary could hear the squeak from his shoes on the polished floors as he rocked back and forth on his heels.

She tried to ignore him while attempting to make sense of the man she'd bumped into. However, her mind was flooded with thoughts she could not control, not least her imminent arrest and all that would mean. But as the argument reached a new and higher pitch, it drew her attention. It was not a good sign. As panic washed over her, she felt hot and nauseous.

The policeman sniggered again.

'All right,' Mary snapped. 'What's so funny?'

'*Sergeant* O'Connor. Sounds nice, don't it?' The policeman gave a broad smile as he rocked again on his heels, his hands behind his back, his head tilted up to the ceiling. 'Sergeant O'Connor!' He nodded with satisfaction. 'You're my ticket, Finch, to a pay rise and stripes.'

'For wrongful arrest? See if I don't sue. Then what would they do with your stripes?'

'You need a snipe for that. Know many lawyers, *do we*?'

Mary grumped. She knew no one, other than Emma Watkins and the Dibbles, who owned a pie shop in Baker Street, let alone a lawyer. She was acting bravely and no more. It was slowly dawning on her not only that she was in trouble, but just how much trouble that was.

'What'll happen now?' Mary asked timidly.

The policeman gave her an astonished look and she fidgeted nervously under his firm gaze.

'I'll take you to Bow Street, and you'll be charged – what do you think will happen? Why did you do it, Finch? After everything those good people have done for you. You must be such a disappointment to them. *Such a disappointment,*' O'Connor echoed Mr Grimwig's pronouncement, much to her annoyance. 'If you own up, the judge will go light on you.'

Mary ground her teeth. She was more irritated than ashamed. Closing her eyes and taking a deep breath did not help; she felt like she could happily thump someone, she was so angry. However, she had enough problems already. So, she stayed quiet while Constable O'Connor continued to smile and rock happily back and forth.

Somewhere upstairs, the triplets were arguing about the sweets, just as Mary had known they would, their voices as shrill as their mother's. She pursed her mouth tightly – the nails were dragging down the blackboard.

By now, the argument from the drawing room had reached a new pitch. This was unheard of, especially as Mr Boots was involved – the butler arguing with his employer? On occasion, it seemed everyone in the room was speaking at the same time.

Then Mr Grimwig bellowed, 'Enough!' and suddenly, the argument stopped. The unexpected silence drew Mary and the policeman's attention to the locked door of the drawing room. A heavy quiet had descended, but her ears were filled with the thumping beats of her heart.

Mary glanced at Constable O'Connor. He still wore his self-satisfied smirk.

The drawing room door opened. Mr Grimwig and Mr Boots stepped out. Behind them, Mrs Grimwig's face was like thunder, and it went through several twist and turns to arrive at something that looked normal. Her husband, though, was calm and serene. And Mr Boots was inscrutable as ever.

Mr Grimwig walked forward slowly, deep in contemplation, and Mary held her breath. Her thoughts raced. She readied herself to receive the bad news his wife's dark glower had suggested was coming.

'Well, Mary Finch…' Mr Grimwig said.

Her heart sank as a knot tightened in her stomach and a lump filled her throat. In her mind's eye, she watched herself being marched away to jail.

'…it seems you are a lucky girl,' Mr Grimwig continued with a soft and controlled voice. 'Constable, my wife and I have decided we shall not be pressing charges–'

'Not… press… charges?' the policeman stammered in astonishment.

Mary was equally taken aback. She stood wide-eyed in disbelief. *What did he just say?* she asked herself.

'No. As my wife has pointed out…' Dora Grimwig was about to say something, but he stepped in front of her, '…the jewels have been returned, and since Mary is an orphan who has led a harsh life–'

'Not… press… charges? Sir?'

'We have a social and Christian duty and we feel Mary must be given a second chance.'

'Not–'

'I believe you heard me correctly, Constable,' said Mr Grimwig.

'Sir!' Mary said in a shrill voice. 'Sir… I mean… thank you… sir!'

Her mouth opened and closed like a fish's and little more sound came from her as she struggled to comprehend what she had just heard. Her world, which had been turned upside down, was turned right ways back again. As her heart fluttered wildly, she felt breathless. It was all she could do not to heave a sigh of relief. She looked at Mr Grimwig and Mr Boots, unable to conceal her wide smile of joy.

Constable O'Connor, though, stood gawping. Seeing his reflection in the hall mirror, disappointment at his vanishing promotion hopes written all over his face, he quickly took on an attitude of respectful professionalism.

He spluttered and stuttered before answering contritely. 'Yes, sir. I understand, sir,' while standing to attention and not understanding at all.

'However, it would be remiss if there were no punishment, Mary.' Mr Grimwig turned his attention back to the scullery maid and his face became stern. 'For you to profit from the experience, we feel you cannot remain in our employment. You will leave. And you will do so tonight.'

Mary's heart caught in her throat. She stared at him in disbelief. She trembled and gasped and finally managed to stutter, 'But, sir, this ain't fair, sir. I didn't do anything, sir.'

She reached out to grasp his hand, but Mr Grimwig drew back.

'Our judgment is not harsh.' He said this in a soft, contrite manner as if he was speaking to an infant and his pronouncement pained him. 'Given the circumstance, it is fair. I'll not have any more discussion on the matter. My mind is quite made up.'

Mrs Grimwig pushed Mr Boots aside and came to stand beside her husband. She lifted her head haughtily and said, 'We ain't…' she caught herself and her lips twitched in annoyance. Taking pains to pronounce each word clearly, she said, 'We *are not* pressing charges, so no crime has been committed as far as we are concerned.'

'Boots,' Mr Grimwig said sharply, 'see that Mary collects her belongings and is gone within the hour.'

He turned to the policeman. A pleasant, friendly warmth came into his voice as he reached out his arm to place it around O'Connor's shoulders and draw him closer.

'Thank you, Constable,' he whispered. 'It was a fine job you did. I shall speak to your inspector in the morning and convey my gratitude for the magnificent manner in which you performed your duties. I'm sure we can rely on your discretion to keep this matter quiet.' He winked. 'If the criminal classes were to find out that we were nearly burgled, it might give them ideas to try again. I think mum's the word, don't you agree, Constable?' He tapped his nose with a finger.

Before Constable O'Connor could answer, Mr Grimwig turned, gripped his wife's arm and led her back to the drawing room. It was left to Mr Boots to escort a disappointed policeman to the front door.

When he returned he growled at Mary, 'Pack your things, Finch.'

There was something about Mr Boots, some hidden undercurrent that had always frightened her. She saw it again in the cold harshness of the butler's unyielding gaze and heard it in the bluntness of his voice.

'But, Mr Boots – it's snowing and the middle of the night… if I have to go, can't I go in the morning?'

'Tonight means tonight. And it's stopped snowing,' he said. 'You're lucky the master is in a good mood otherwise you'd be spending your nights in Bow Street nick. You've an hour. And I'll be outside the door, just in case those fingers decide to wander.'

5

MARY FINCH, EMMA WATKINS AND MR BOOTS

Mary surveyed her tiny attic room and sighed. It wasn't much. There was a small cot; the mattress was lumpy, but still comfortable. A chest of drawers stood by the window. She had placed a patterned napkin rescued from the rag-and-bone man on top of it, along with her hairbrush, a small free-standing mirror and a candle in a holder. The penny dreadful magazine she was reading was on a corner, as was one of her most treasured possession, a book: *The Adventures of Sherlock Holmes.* It was a collection of short stories given to her by Dr Watson himself, no less. He had even signed it:

To Mary Finch,

for your help in solving the Boat Train mystery,

from Dr J H Watson and Sherlock Holmes.

Beside the chest of drawers was a rickety chair and

behind them both was the window with its magnificent view across the park. In summer, she could daydream, watching the ladies, their children and nannies, picnicking far below under the dappled shade of tall trees. She always felt as if she was perched high above the world with London stretched out and resting beneath her, waiting for a command from Lady Mary Finch.

Beside the book there was a photograph of Mary with her father, mother and her brother, Danny, who was four years older than her. Her father and mother looked proudly out of the picture. How old was she when they sat for the photograph? Three? Probably. She barely remembered it, just as she barely remembered them.

She shivered at the memory of a dream of cold water, a vague recollection of the accident that had claimed her parents' lives. In the dream, she was desperately frightened, thrashing about, calling their names, but no one answered and she never saw them again. That was the day when everything changed. That was the day she lost her parents and soon after, she was to lose Danny. And now she was about to lose this life, too. Once again, she was going to be cast adrift.

Mary reminded herself that she was strong. She had survived worse and she was determined to survive this: she would not be cowered.

She carefully wrapped the photograph and frame in a blouse and placed it on the bed. Of the very few souvenirs she had of the past, this one was far too precious and needed treating kindly.

Removing one of the pillowcases, she began to place her clothes and things inside. She had no bag, so that would have to suffice. She didn't think Mr Grimwig would mind. It wasn't long before she'd cleared everything.

There were three small prints on the wall (posters advertising productions at the Gaiety Theatre, the Royalty and Weston's Music Hall that brightened up the room). She decided to leave them for the next scullery maid. This room would become hers.

Finally, Mary sat on the chair and looked at her reflection in the small mirror. She adjusted her hair and gave it a sharp, angry swipe before putting the brush inside the pillowcase. She was sad she could not say a proper goodbye to those she knew.

By now, the cat was awake and sitting on the bed, watching her. For a moment, Mary believed he could sense something was amiss. But then Oscar yawned. He lifted his paw, licked it with his pink sandpaper tongue and began to wash his head with it, ignoring her completely.

'I can't take you,' she said.

She chewed her lips and shook back the tears. Everything was packed. It was no use worrying about the unfairness of her situation. She might as well rant at the moon. She could not stay – it was as simple as that. The night was cold and there was a chilly walk to look forward to.

Mary took a deep breath and gave a long sigh.

'You just be kind to the next maid,' she told the cat. 'Keep her warm at night, like you did me. You listening? You're better than a hot water bottle, you are. But I'll come back for you. Honest, I will.'

There was a soft rap on the door. Emma slipped in, looking frightened.

'What's going on?' Mary asked.

'Wh-who was the man you bumped into?' Emma asked cautiously.

Mary glared at her, more out of disbelief than anger.

'You well know who it was, Emma Watkins,' she hissed and pointed a finger at her. 'I saw that look you gave me. Ain't Boots outside?'

Emma shook her head. 'He's downstairs in the kitchen with the cooking sherry.'

'Oi! What's this?' Mary brushed the hair away from Emma's face. On the maid's cheek was a small red bruise, quickly blackening. 'How'd you get that?'

Emma pulled away and adjusted her hair to conceal the mark. She looked guilty, her eyes dropping to the floor.

'Bumped the door,' she mumbled.

'Bump…?' Mary gave her a long hard stare. She pursed her lips angrily. 'Him? The thief? He did that?'

'Davey? No, no, no, honestly, it wasn't Davey,' Emma said a little too quickly for Mary's liking.

Mary crooked her neck and watched her friend carefully. Even though she was three years younger than Emma, she always felt three years older.

'You telling me the truth?'

Emma nodded dumbly and reached for Mary's hand.

'I don't believe you for one second.' Mary pulled her hand away. 'It was him I saw leaving the house, wasn't it? Did you know he was going to steal her jewels?' She saw Emma flinch. 'You better not lie to me, Watkins.'

'Honest, Mary, I didn't… I-I-I–' Emma shied away from the frown Mary gave her. 'God's truth, Mary, I swear I ain't lying! Cross my heart!' Which she did. 'Honest. Y-y-you ain't gonna tell Mr G, are you?' she said hesitantly. 'That me and Davey is seeing each other? I-I-I…I mean, not after all I've done for you.'

'Done for me?' Mary looked puzzled. 'What you on about?'

'Looked after you… like me and cook did when you first came, and… helping you… with Mr Boots… Please, Mary–' she was unable to conceal her fears.

Mary pursed her lips and shook her head in frustration. She was annoyed that her friend would question her loyalty. How easy it would have been to say what little she knew and maybe save herself from being fired. But even then, she knew better.

'Tell them?' she said. 'Don't be daft.'

She sighed. Emma had not lied – she did not know he would try to steal Mrs Grimwig's jewels, of that Mary was certain. She smiled and shook her head, understanding the girl's worries.

'Telling them ain't gonna help anyone,' she said. 'I'm caught either way, don't you see? If I say I know *him,* then I'd be really up for the high jump. Then they'd believe him and me were in it together and I'd definitely be going to jail. And what can I tell them? Nothing, 'caus I don't know nothing to tell, other than *you* knew him.' Emma's mouth fell open. 'And if I tell them that, it'll still be the same, except we'd both be on our way to Bow Street with *Sergeant* O'Connor. They'd only go and think all of us were in it together. This way, at least one of us still has her job.'

A tight smile of relief appeared on Emma's worried face. Mary brushed the maid's hair away from the bruise.

'Bumped the door, my aunt…' she muttered, huffed and turned on her heels to gaze out the window into the night. She took a deep breath to calm herself. In her mind's eye, she saw the thief raise his fist to strike her, the menace that lurked behind his dark eyes. Her mind raced. How strangely Mr Grimwig had acted. He, his wife and Boots were quarrelling in the drawing room, going at it hammer and tongs – she'd never heard of anything like that before. Master and servant arguing! That she did not understand. At least all the charges against her had been dropped.

'Where're you gonna go?' Emma asked quietly.

Mary shook her head to clear her mind.

'To my friends' house in Baker Street.' Mary sounded confident when in truth she was nervous, but she wasn't going to give in to self-pity and fear. 'Grandma and Grandpa Dibble will put me up until I can get myself fixed.'

Emma started to cry. Mary reached over and drew the girl closer, knowing the tears were ones of relief rather than anything else. But she didn't mind; they were still friends. There was no point in being angry.

'Come on, Ems, don't you start that blubbing. You'll get me at it if you do. It's done. I ain't going to jail, no matter what that copper said. He'll be *Sergeant* O'Connor in a month of Sundays. But your Davey's put me in Queer Street good and proper. When the word gets around, how am I gonna find another position in as good a house as this? Who'd hire a thief?'

Mary winked. 'But no one's got the better of *Lady Mary Finch* yet,' she said and saw a smile break Emma's lips. 'That's better. Now, about Davey–'

Mary broke off when a sudden knock on the door startled them both. Almost immediately, the door swung back and Mr Boots stood there, red-faced, drunk and swaying.

'What's this, then? A conspiracy, is it?' he slurred, his breath smelling strongly of sherry. Both girls stiffened and Oscar disappeared under the bed.

'What are you doing here, Watkins?'

'She's saying goodbye, Mr Boots, that's all,' Mary said quickly.

Mr Boot's eyes wandered menacingly between the two girls.

'Get off back to your room, Watkins,' he sneered. 'Since you're such close pals, you get Mary's duties until we can hire another scullery maid. You remember what they are, don't you?' He gave her a black look.

Emma left with a nervous glance back.

'Well? Got your things?' Mr Boots asked. 'Do I need to check them to see if you've lifted anything?'

Mary held the pillowcase closely and saw a strange smile curl Mr Boot's lips. She held it out reluctantly, half expecting the butler to empty it and check the contents thoroughly. But Mr Boots took it, sniffed haughtily and handed it straight back.

'Apparently, we can't have you arrested, can we?' he said, making no attempt to conceal his disdain. 'Not tonight, at any rate, according to *His Honourable Lordship,* Mr Grimwig.'

'What do you mean?' Mary asked.

'But if I had my way…' he said slowly and the darkness returned to his face. Mary shuddered at the threat behind the look.

He held the bedroom door open. With a flick of his head, he indicated that she should leave.

'You mark my words, Finch. This ain't over, not by a long chalk,' he mumbled as she walked past. 'Maybe there'll be work for Mr Grimwig's lawyer, after all.'

A nervous shiver ran down Mary's spine.

6

A FIGURE IN THE DARK

It had indeed stopped snowing. As Mary stood on the front steps, she gave a regretful smile. She'd entered the Grimwigs' house three years ago by the servants' entrance at the back, and now she was leaving through the front door. However, it wasn't quite the advancement it might appear to be.

While the Grimwigs were not the ideal employers, they were better than her previous ones – Mrs Fortesque and her son were worse by far – and she was sad to leave. As she stepped on to the pavement, she sighed and looked back to where she and the thief had crashed. Fresh snow had completely covered the ground, erasing any signs of the collision.

'It would have been so easy, *Sergeant* O'Connor,' Mary mused, 'if you'd just followed his trail and caught him.'

Mary took one last look at the closed front door. The moment reminded her of something Sherlock Holmes had once said: this was a dramatic moment of fate, when you hear a step on the stairs walking into your life, and you don't know whether it's for good or ill.

She turned, and with a heavy heart, *Lady Mary Finch* walked away.

There was something magical about the streets that night. The air had become icy and still; there was not a hint of a breeze. All smelled fresh and clean. The snow had softened all the contours of the street, and it was impossible to tell where the pavement ended and the road began. The street lamps illuminated the world like spotlights on a theatre stage and the dark houses were elaborate sets for a play. The quiet was deafening broken only by the squeak of the snow under her feet as she walked. It felt like the hush just as the curtains went up.

Mary clutched the pillowcase that held her treasures. Her fingers tingled with excitement. She was worried, though, about having to go back to the Dibbles. After all her efforts, it seemed a step backwards, yet where else could she go? She knew of no other who would take her in.

Her stomach gurgled a complaint – she had missed both tea and dinner. It reminded her of the day she first stood outside the Dibbles' pie shop, nearly three years ago when she was barely ten. Then she hadn't eaten for a day and a half.

SHE HAD JUST RUN AWAY FROM HER EMPLOYERS, THE Fortesques, and had been wandering the streets aimlessly, almost at the point of tears and desperately hungry. The pies in Archimedes Dibble's Pie Shop had seemed so enticing, the smells even more so, making her mouth water and her stomach rumble. The cut behind her ear, given to her by Mrs Fortesque, throbbed horribly.

Mary remembered spending an age deliberating, worried and afraid, until her gurgling stomach made her mind up for her. Having no money, she crept in with one of the customers, reached out, grabbed a pie and made a dash through the door. She had gone no more than twenty feet before bumping into a stout gentleman who was talking to a tall, lean man and rebounding into the arms of Mr Dibble's grandson, Archibald, who was chasing her. She cried out in pain, pretending to have hurt her ankle to solicit sympathy.

Mary smiled, remembering.

She must have appeared a sight. With tattered dress, dirty face, snotty nose, wild and unkempt hair, she would have looked every bit the savage she seemed to be.

'Little thieving…' Archibald swore. 'Honest folks

work for a living. Grandma slaves every day over a hot stove and don't deserve to get robbed.'

He raised his hand to smack her. As Mary tried to scramble away, the gentleman she'd run into grabbed her firmly.

At that moment, Grandpa Dibble appeared. He pushed his grandson's hand away and stood over her. Mary waited for the inevitable hard smack, like the ones she had become so accustomed to during her time with Mrs Fortesque. She stared up defiantly. With mouth set firm and eyes screwed up, she balled her little hands into fists, raised them, tensed her body and glared fiercely.

'Let me go,' she shouted. 'Or I'll bash you.'

At that, the gentleman and Grandpa Dibble burst out laughing.

'A veritable spitfire,' the gentleman said, 'if ever I saw one.'

'Not one to mess with, sir.'

'I think even Mr Sullivan, the Boston Strong Boy, might find her a handful.'

'Oh! I'd not go fifteen rounds with this one, not even for sport, that's for sure.'

'Come, child, let's see if any damage has been done. Can we use your shop as a surgery, Mr Dibble?'

'Of course, Dr Watson. Archie, carry Bare-knuckles Jessie to the back room and watch she don't *bash you.'*

Mary scowled but allowed the boy to lift her. She

glanced up to the person standing behind the stout gentleman, a man, with silent, hawk-like grey eyes.

Afterwards, to her surprise, Grandpa Dibble did not take her to the workhouse as she had expected, but instead found her a bed under the counter in the shop. Soon, she became friends with the whole family, and especially with Archie. He was three-years-older than Mary and was big for his age – she once joked, he was a testament to how good his grandma's pies were.

For the month she was with them, she helped to look after Dot and Sally – Sossie as the family called her – the youngest of the Dibbles, served in the shop, cleaned and washed up – a general dogsbody. But it was the happiest she had been from since when she could not remember.

At the end of the month, Archie's grandmother bought her a dress from a second-hand shop. She made sure Mary washed her face, tidied her hair and blew her nose on a handkerchief. They walked over to a house in Regent's Park, where Mary was to be the scullery maid. Emma Watkins was to be her mentor.

So, she started her job with the Grimwigs. Poorly paid, long, hard hours, but a job, and it came with the attic room she so loved. She even made a new friend – Oscar, the failed mouser.

Mary turned into Marylebone, still deep in thought. The street was empty at this late hour. She felt the cold biting and walked quickly along.

Something was nagging her. A feeling she could not place gave her cause to glance back. Someone was following her. At first, she thought she was mistaken. But when she turned again to get a better view, she saw him duck into the frozen gloom beyond the streetlights.

She waited to see if he would emerge. When he didn't, she felt the cold nipping her nose and carried on walking, more quickly now. Anxiously, she glanced behind as she hurried along.

She saw him. He was some way back, a dark figure slipping in and out of the shadows, keeping his distance.

Soon, she was running. She fancied he was coming after her, and thought she could hear his feet crunching into the fresh snow. She clutched her bundle tighter and fled, fearful that the thief was chasing her to regain his spoils. Spots danced in front of her eyes as her heart thumped painfully in her chest. With panic rising inside, a sickening flood threatening to overwhelm her, she turned into Baker Street.

Somewhere, a bell chimed twelve clear notes that rang keenly in the cold night air. By then, Mary was standing in front of Archimedes Dibble's Pie Shop. Panting hard, her breath a frosty mist in the air, she pounded on the door with balled fists and leant heavily against it, all the while casting a troubled, anxious gaze behind her.

She could not see him, whoever it was. But she could feel his eyes from somewhere in the shadows, spying on her. The windows of the shops and houses on Baker Street were all dark. All except those of number 221b, where Sherlock Holmes was burning the midnight oil.

7

THAT NIGHT AND THE NEXT DAY

In the snowy quiet, it sounded as if she had struck the door with a hammer. She had to knock several times hoping that whoever was following her would not suddenly appear. She waited impatiently, stamping her aching feet to warm them up, gulping air to get her breath back, her quick eyes scanning the street.

Through the darkened window, Mary spied someone with a candle enter the shop. She could see the flickering light, shielded by a hand. As it came nearer a face appeared at the window. A dark-haired, stocky, well-built boy of sixteen years peeped out. It was Archibald Socrates Dibble.

'Who's there?' he whispered loudly. 'What do you want?'

'Archie, it's me. Mary,' she shouted. 'Quick, let me in.'

‘Mary? What’s going on? It’s gone midnight.’

The bolts complained noisily as he drew them back.

Archie looked tired as he squinted at her with a puzzled expression. ‘Well, you do look a sight–’

In an instant, Mary tried to squeeze past him, almost pushing him to the ground.

‘Whoa. Hold your horses,’ Archie grabbed her. ‘What’s up with you?’

‘Someone’s following me,’ she whispered urgently and glanced behind her.

‘What you on about?’ Archie said. He gave Mary a curious stare, and then stepped out into the street. He peered into the darkness as Mary peeped around his shoulders. The street was empty. There were only Mary’s footprints in the snow leading up to the door, and they went back until they vanished in the gloom – no others could be seen.

‘Ain’t no one about,’ Archie said and shivered in the cold night air.

‘Can I come in?’ Mary said.

‘Blimey! You look like death warmed up.’ He laughed. Mary saw her reflection in the glass of the door. It was a pathetic sight: a girl with unkempt hair, not unlike how she’d looked the first time they’d met. ‘Of course you can. Come on. It’s bleedin’ cold.’

Even as she entered the shop, Mary took one last look behind her. She felt the hair on her arms rise. Whoever was watching, she was sure, was still there, hidden and mysterious.

The shop lay in deep shadow. The cold light from the streetlamps fell through the windows and gleamed off the polished tabletops. At the back of the shop, in the dark rectangle of a doorway, Sally Dibble stood in her white nightdress, her arms folded tightly across her chest to ward off the cold. The eight-year-old yawned and raised her knuckles to rub her sleepy eyes.

'Who's there, Archie?' she asked.

'It's Mary,' Archie replied. 'Go back to bed, Sossie.'

'Hello, Mary.' She yawned again. 'What you doing here?'

'Get back to bed, Sossie. Hurry now,' Archie said

Sally turned and began to dawdle up the stairs.

'Hurry, I said.'

'I'm going as fast as I can. I'm only little.'

'Hurry, or Jack will get you.'

Sally yelped and dashed up the stairs out of sight.

In the kitchen, Mary tried to explain what had happened. But she was tired. Now that the excitement was over, she felt washed out. The day had caught up with her and she stumbled over her words.

'Come on,' Archie said. 'Leave it till tomorrow. You need to sleep.'

'If you get me a blanket, Archie,' Mary said, 'I'll curl up under the counter like the old days.'

'Under the counter, my what's it! Let's get you a proper bed. You can sleep in the upstairs storeroom tonight. It's got a bed in it now, and a set of drawers.'

The room was small with a window at the end, the bare floor cleared and swept. Mary lay uncomfortably in the bed, missing the slight weight of Oscar against her legs and worrying. Despite her tiredness, her mind refused to rest, and it played through the events of the night in a continuous loop.

This is not over, she thought. Not with someone following her. Moreover, she worried that Mr Grimwig could simply change his mind. She had the distinct feeling that he had a reason for letting her go that wasn't the least bit charitable. And in that same easy way he'd allowed her to go, he could just as easily have her arrested. Was that what the butler's parting words about lawyers meant?

Such fears for her freedom mingled with doubts about just how would she get another position – even with Grandma Dibble's help. What other skills did she have? She was a maid and nothing else. And she couldn't stay with the Dibbles forever.

The Dibbles, though, were kind people. The pie shop had a good reputation and was often busy. Grandma's pies were sought after (Mrs Hudson from along the street shopped there and even Mr Holmes occasionally dropped in). Mary felt lucky that she knew them.

But luck was an up and down thing, she considered, a fickle friend. A few minutes earlier, or later, and she would have missed Davey, Emma's *amour.* Then no one would have thought her a crook and she'd still have her job, even though Mrs Grimwig would have lost her gems. But it was the way of things, that *Lady Mary Finch* should have been there at that very moment.

Her sleep, when it came, was fitful and suffused with strange dreams. At one point she stirred and startled; a frightful shape swam out of the blackness to hover over her. She half-opened her eyes, and then did so completely in a panic – a face hung over her as if dangling on a string, and it looked like the thief. She reached out in a fright to grasp it, and it was gone.

She sat up in bed, drenched in sweat and shivering in the icy air of the unheated room. There was dead silence everywhere. Then she heard the twisting of the doorknob. She shuddered and tensed herself. Quietly, she slipped deeper under the blankets, holding her breath.

The door opened a crack and in the darkness she heard Archie's voice.

'Mary, you all right?' he whispered.

She mumbled something and went even further under her blankets, curled up her legs, wrapped her arms around her knees and slept fitfully again.

She awoke after her restless night to the sight of Sally Dibble standing over her with a steaming cup of tea.

Archie was behind her with a slice of bread in a saucer. Mary smiled at the royal treatment – tea in bed, and at such a late hour.

She sat up, drawing the blanket around her tightly; her breath was a mist in the cold air and she wrapped her hands around the warm teacup and sighed loudly. The events of the previous night washed through her mind as she talked them over with Archie and left her as puzzled now as she had been then.

'I don't get it,' Mary said. 'I mean, Mrs G could see that all her jewels were there when her husband tipped them out. He told her as much. But she started going on about how I was to give them back. "Where are they?" she yelled at me. They were all there, in front of her eyes. Was she blind? Look, Archie, don't ask me why, but I had the impression that Mrs G was looking for something else besides her jewels.'

'Like what?'

Mary shrugged. 'I don't know. It's just how she acted. And why didn't Mr G have me arrested? I mean, he was so convinced I was a thief–'

'–and you and this Davey was in it together.'

Mary nodded. 'Instead, he just lets me go. It doesn't make sense.'

'Well, he's rich enough to do that, ain't he?'

'That's something else I've always wondered about. Just how did the Grimwigs get so rich so quickly?'

'Luck, I guess. Owning a mill helps.'

'And how did they get that? Luck? One step from the poorhouse to a mansion on Regent's Park isn't just all luck.'

Archie shrugged. 'What's brought this on?' he asked.

Mary bit her lips and exhaled a small groan.

'What happened,' she said, ' and how they all acted, and being followed is what. All that quarrelling. It's got me wondering again.'

Archie laughed. 'You read too many Penny Dreadfuls.'

Mary huffed. 'I didn't imagine being followed last night, Archie. I didn't! I thought it was the thief, Davey. But why would he want to follow me? I don't have the gems – he must have figured that out. If it wasn't him, then who was it?' She sipped her tea, closed her eyes and said softly, 'I had a thought when I woke up – that it might have been…' She shrugged, wrapped her arms around her legs, and rested her chin on her knees and gazed down at the blankets.

Archie looked at her and smiled. 'Much too many, for sure–'

'It's just a feeling I had,' she said and pursed her lips. 'I mean, last night was odd. Why did they just fire me? Then Mr Boots said something like it wouldn't do to have me arrested, at least not yet… and then…'

'Come on,' he said with a broad smile, 'it's over. It's

all done. You're free, ain't you? We just got to find you a job.'

'No, seriously, Archie. What did he mean by that?' Mary asked. 'Anyways, who's gonna hire me if they think I'm a crook? So, I can't just sit and do nothing. I need to find Davey to figure out what happened and what he did. Though I'm not sure what I'll do if I find him. It might just get Emma and me into even more trouble. But let's face it, I've got to try to clear my name, or at least figure out what happened last night.'

8

STRANGE MEETINGS

Mary forced such thoughts from her mind. As long as she was with the Dibbles, she was determined to help out and earn her keep. So, when Grandma wanted an errand run to Smithfield Market, Mary volunteered. She was to see Mr Fallows, the only butcher Grandma trusted to supply her with meat. This was ideal. Doing something would at least stop last night's events from endlessly repeating themselves in her mind.

Her plan was to walk to the top of Baker Street, into Oxford Street, past Mr Marshall's sweet shop and along towards Holborn and Farringdon. She looked at her shoes and could already feel the damp penetrating the thin soles. By the time she returned, she would have wet and frozen feet. Mary adjusted her shawl and the coat

Grandma Dibble had loaned her, readying herself for the journey.

Already, after less than a day, the snow on the road was rutted and yellowish, swiftly being turned into a muddy slush by the wheels of the carriages or where the hoofs of the horses had trampled it. The air was icy. Solitary pigeons, gaunt and silent, like silver-grey-green gargoyles, perched on high sills, were fluffed up against the weather. Above them, the sky was cloudy. Without the brightness of the sun, the light was flat and dull.

Baker Street was busy with carriages weaving and manoeuvring in a complicated dance. The omnibuses clanked and the horses' smoky snorting breath erupted like steam escaping from a pipe as they dragged the heavy vehicles along. People crowded the pavements, bustling here and there, going to work or home. Barrows trundled past. Hawkers screamed their wares. Three labourers working on the road opposite the pie shop warmed their hands over a fire melting tar. A child was crying, stamping his feet and shouting he wanted the blue one. His mother wearily handed several brightly wrapped parcels to a maid. Just along from Mary, a red-nosed elderly lady in a heavy dark coat was shouting, 'Gypsy charms! Gypsy charms! Brings you luck!' The tray she clutched was full of sprigs of dried purple flowers wrapped in bundles as tightly as she was wrapped in her coat. Next to her, a small girl cried, 'Matches! Matches!' as they headed towards Oxford Street.

Mary picked a sprig from the tray and gave the old lady a penny. 'I need a bit of luck!' she said. Crouching down, she took some matches from the small girl. 'I need some of these as well.' When she handed over a coin, the girl's face brightened with a rosy smile.

As Mary threaded the flowers into a buttonhole, she noticed Mr Boots. The memories of last night returned. He was advancing slowly, his eyes fixed on her. She was thinking about crossing the street – the butler was the last person she wanted to meet – when a carriage drew up alongside. The black horse neighed loudly, his flanks steaming as he stamped his hoof hard against the cobble-stone with a resounding thump. Sparks flew from his metal shoe.

The blinds of the carriage were parted and a well-dressed man in his fifties leaned out, what seemed to be an intellectual face held in a frozen smile. He looked officious. His grey eyes gleamed brightly behind gold-rimmed glasses.

'Mary Finch? You are she?' he asked in a smooth and suave voice, smiling as if he already knew the answer and was just being polite. 'Audacious, I must say. Foolish, but audacious.' He nodded.

Mary's brow furrowed. 'Sir?'

'But getting caught… Hmmm! Well, not so good.' He

sighed, shook his head solemnly, and watched her over the rim of his glasses. 'It was greed, of course, you do know that? That is what did you both.'

Mary paused for a second and recalled Mr Boots's words. She glanced over towards the butler and gave him a contemptuous glare.

'I didn't take them,' Mary said to the gentleman. 'Mr Grimwig has already fired me for something I didn't do, and he's got his jewels back, so I would appreciate it if both you and he would leave me be.'

'Quite so, I am sure – but it is something *he* is hardly likely to do,' the gentleman continued matter-of-factly. 'I was just commenting that one should have kept one's eyes on the prize and not got distracted.'

'Prize?' Mary looked at him and then over to Mr Boots.

Noticing him, the gentleman smiled politely, touched his hat with the handle of his cane and gave him a single nod. Mr Boots, though, watched them with an oddly puzzled look. The gentleman tapped his nose with a finger.

'I understand. I take it that you are the… shall we say, brains?' He gave a slight laugh. 'It was obviously not your friend.'

'Brains?'

'Forgive my rudeness; it was uncalled for. But it seems as if your friend has played us both and he is…

what shall we say? He is in the wind. And he has left you holding the bag, figuratively speaking.' A change came over the gentleman, an edge came to his voice. 'I have lost a good night's sleep over this affair, Miss Finch. It would be better if you could find him… for everyone's sake. Certainly for yours. And before the law is further involved. I do not think you would like that. It is not nice being made a fool of, is it? My card.'

In his plump hand, he held a small white card and pushed it forward. Mary instinctively reached out and took it.

'When you are ready, by all means come around,' he said. 'The sooner we can conclude business, the better, and you will find me very generous. Good day, Miss Finch, I look forward to seeing you – and your friend. Soon I hope.'

He gave another slight nod to Mr Boots, then tapped the roof of his carriage with his cane. The driver clucked, snapped the reins and the horse sprang away.

'But, sir…' Mary shouted after him.

As the carriage passed the butler, the curtains were flicked shut. Mr Boots stared at it as it made its way along to Marylebone Road. Then he turned towards Mary, moved forward mechanically and purposefully, only to hesitate and stop as if caught between two worlds. His eyes flicked continuously between Mary and the carriage. He seemed confused.

Mary quickly placed the card inside her pocket.

'I warned you–' Mr Boots started to say, but before he had time to finish, Mary, whose pulse was racing, spoke angrily.

'So, who else has he told? Does everyone know? How am I meant to get a job if he's told everyone? I thought Mr Grimwig said it was all over – was it you who got him to set his snipe on me?'

She gulped in surprise at her boldness, then drew back in horror as she saw a knot of muscle tremble in the butler's jaw.

'What the hell are you talking about?' Mr Boots barked. 'Now, you listen to me–' He grabbed her wrist and twisted her arm. 'You'd do well to choose your friends better,' he growled. His face was hovering menacingly close; his breath was in her face and she winced in pain. 'This changes things, Finch, you know that, don't you? I warned you this wasn't over. You better tell that friend of yours: if he thinks this is a game, let's see if he likes playing by my rules.'

Several people had stopped to watch the sudden commotion. Mary attempted to squirm away.

'But the snipe said…'

'Don't act the fool with me,' Boots bellowed.

'Sir!' a young man shouted and began to move closer. Mr Boots glared at the man. But when he saw others were looking at him – several people, in fact, all watching him intently – the darkness left his face to be replaced by a forced thin-lipped smile. Seeming to remember who he was – butler to Mr Grimwig of Regent's Park – he released Mary's wrist and fumbled awkwardly in a pocket. He took out some coins, almost dropping them in his hurry, and, smiling at the crowd, turned back to Mary.

'Your back wages…' he said loudly so all could hear, 'for the week… Mr Grimwig thought… have it…'

Mary was startled. 'Wages? Mr Boots, I didn't expect–'

He made a show of slapping the coins into her open hand.

'Four and six? Mr Boots… but that's too much–'

'Mr Grimwig's a fair man!' he said loudly.

Hearing this, and seeing the money in her hand, the young man stopped his advance a few paces short of them. He hesitated, and he gave a polite nod to Mary, turned and moved away. Those who had just been watching did the same.

Mr Boots gave them, and particularly the young man, a contemptuous scowl, then leant close to Mary.

'You and your friend think you're clever, little girl? You better wake up, Finch, before it's too late!'

With that, he stormed off, muttering expletives.

'Mr Boots! I don't understand.' Mary ran after him, but the butler pushed his way through the crowd, leaving her behind. 'I don't know who the man I bumped into was,' Mary shouted. 'He's no friend of mine – nor's the lawyer. I never met them before. Mr Boots, I was chasing after the thief like you and everyone else…'

And then she fell silent. She rubbed her wrist. She was so angry that her heart thrummed loudly in her ears. But she was puzzled, too. The fine gentleman, what was his name? She looked at the card: Milverton. He was talking in riddles. What business? What prize? What a strange lawyer. Though what was strange or normal for a man in that profession, she did not know. And though Mr Boots knew him, the butler appeared flustered and unusually perturbed by his appearance. And even he was speaking in riddles.

This affair, however, despite what Mr Grimwig had said, was far from finished, of that she was certain now that a lawyer was involved. Things had changed, Mr Boots said. Though what had changed, and what had changed them, she did not know.

She looked at the three coins in her hand. Well, maybe *her* luck had changed. The lucky sprig had cost her a penny and she'd made four and six.

As she walked towards Oxford Street, she stopped and swung around on her heels, glancing back the way the butler had gone.

'Boots,' she whispered. 'How did he know where I was staying? Was he the one following me? Did he think… that I'd lead him to…? Wait a second, ain't today Saturday? Boots don't ever leave the house on Saturdays. Today's about the household accounts, polishing silver, getting things ready for next week, planning menus and arrangements for visitors and the likes.'

Yet there he had been, arguing with her on Baker Street. She continued walking, but had to stop again, her brow wrinkled.

If it were back wages he wanted to give, why do it himself? It would have been usual to send Emma or a footman to do that – the task was far too menial for a man of his position.

Mary saw Mr Boots clearly in her mind's eye. In the heat of the moment, there was something else she had not noticed: he had been sweating. He hadn't even shaved. His clothes were creased as if he had slept in them. And that was so unlike him – arguing in public.

9

THE INCIDENT WITH THE HANSOM AND THE SCAR-FACED MAN

Smithfield was just as she remembered it: busy, noisy and smelly. Thousands of carcasses hung on hooks, and though Mary wasn't squeamish, the sheer volume of death made her nauseous. She wandered among the many stalls and corners in search of Mr Fallows while the discordant din of the market assaulted her ears. Whistling, barking, grunts and shouts, quarrelling and haggling, chopping all echoed beneath the roof of the vast building, while porters pushed and pulled trolleys and heaved whole sheep and legs of cows with consummate ease. Mary screwed her nose up and wondered how people could work there.

Mary found Mr Fallows quickly enough and was glad she hadn't had to search the whole market. A portly man with a ruddy face, Mr Fallows sported a large blue-veined nose, under which was a bushy greying moustache. He was wearing a blood-streaked apron and leaning across a chopping table with a gore stained cleaver in his hand. His sleeves were rolled up even though the market was a good deal colder than outside.

It was only after she'd concluded her business with the butcher and turned to leave that Mary noticed the stranger watching her. A grubby dishevelled, black-haired man dressed differently from those around him – differently enough for Mary to think he was not one of them – stood back in the shadows. Even with his cap drawn down, shading his face, he could not conceal the livid scar that ran from scalp to chin across his cheek and the glimmer of his strange reddish eye. All around him, people moved briskly and with purpose, yet he stood quite still, and Mary knew it was she he was watching. Last night's fears returned.

She turned to the butcher and asked, 'Mr Fallows, who's that man?'

'What man?' Mr Fallows enquired. When Mary turned back to point, the man had gone.

She left Smithfield quickly, unable to explain her nervousness and fears, and wondering if, amongst all this butchery, she was, after all, just imagining things. So much had happened recently to leave her jittery. As she hurried away, she thought a scarred man would not be an unusual sight, especially in a meat market where accidents must be commonplace, and scars and missing fingers would abound. Yet it was the way he was watching – intently, fixedly – and how he was dressed – no apron or overalls – that marked him out of place. And the scar? Such a livid brand. She wondered how *that* could have happened accidentally.

Passing Chancery Lane, she saw the clerks and the lawyers hurrying to some assize or other; black-attired men, dour, solemn and hawk-like, ready to pick the bones clean at some legal dinner. *So this is where they are,* and she took Milverton's card from her pocket and placed it into her purse. Her near brush with the law had made her acutely aware of the existence of lawyers; she wanted nothing to do with them. But fate seemed determined to push her closer to them. In fact, they seemed to go out of their way to find her.

She walked quickly on and made Oxford Street in no time at all. She had some money now that Mr Boots had paid her, more than she was owed; she could buy a few things for Dot and Sossie as a thank you to Grandpa for taking her in. A book for Dot – she was bound to pass a bookshop – something on… and a… what for Sossie? Something useful. Surely she had outgrown dolls? Mary wasn't sure. No, shoes! That was it! All Sossie ever got was Dot's hand-me-downs. Mary realised she needed a pair herself. Her feet felt chilly and wet from the snow creeping in through the gaps in the soles. And …

As Mary crossed the road, she had finally calmed

down and driven Milverton, Mr Boots and the strange scarred man out of her thoughts. Even so, her head was still in the clouds. Someone was shouting at her. But her thoughts had strayed, and though she could hear the voice, she could not decipher the words.

'Watch out, miss!'

...Sossie hardly ever got anything new...

'Watch out, miss!'

...it would be nice if she could have something she could call her own...

'WATCH OUT!' Finally, the shrill call made her turn.

Mary's legs froze. A hansom cab was bearing down on her. The driver was leaning forward, a scarf drawn across his face, his wild eyes fixed intently on her as he whipped the horse along. Steam erupted from the horse's nostrils as it charged forward. Its wild neighing filled her ears. She felt the wind of the carriage, and then she was tumbling as it flashed past.

She crashed into the snow, the breath driven from her body. Something had barged into her a moment before the horse would have struck and sent her spinning away.

Mary looked up to see the driver furiously whipping the horse as it weaved through the traffic and disappeared around a corner. A crowd of people gathered, some trying to help her up, others standing and looking. Everyone seemed to be talking at the same time.

Are you all right, miss?... Damn, fool!... He could

have killed... Did anyone get his... A doctor... Shall we...? Well done, young lady... Where's a police... Brave, so very brave... The traffic these days...

Mary was dazed and confused and breathless. 'No, I'm fine,' she spluttered. 'Honestly, I'm fine. What happened?'

She stood up on watery legs. A gentleman held her elbow; a woman handed her the basket she'd dropped. Her heart was thumping. The cab had missed her by a fraction only.

Amongst the hubbub, she heard someone crying. The match girl, the one she'd met that morning, was also being helped up, and she was clutching her arm. Her tray had spilled its matches, which lay scattered in the snow. Some passers-by were dusting her down and patting her on the head.

Well done, well done... Splendid... Did you see what she did?... So brave... What a thing... Such a selfless...

Mary gasped and rushed to kneel beside the girl.

'Did you just push me out of the way?'

'Ella! Ella!' the old charm seller shouted, limping as quickly as she could towards them. 'You all right? Ella? Ella?'

'You did, didn't you?' Mary said. She led the girl over to the pavement. 'Bloomin' hell, you saved my life.'

The small girl – it seemed her name was Ella – was

wiping her eyes. She ran to the old woman and folded herself into her dress.

'I'm sorry, Gran, I'm sorry….they're all spoilt…' she cried as her grandmother cuddled her.

'There, there, Ella, you're all right – that's what matters,' her granny said happily.

Mary looked behind her. Ella's matches were being slowly destroyed under the wheels of the carriages. Some flared as the wheels passed over them; most broke or were pressed deeply into the slushy wet snow. The busy traffic dashed any chance of retrieving those not damaged. Oxford Street was teaming once more.

Mary went over to where the two were. The old woman continued soothing the girl, but still Ella wept and rubbed her eyes. Around them, life had returned to normal. The incident was over and people continued their journeys, oblivious to them and what had just happened.

'What a brave thing to do,' Mary said. She leaned over and cuddled the girl. 'Here, you're not hurt, are you?' She felt Ella's arm. The girl shook her head, but was crying too much to reply. 'Cor! Thanks, Ella. I'd be dead if it wasn't for you.' Mary looked back. 'And all your matches ruined!'

She reached inside her pocket and took out a florin, and noticed her fingers were trembling.

'Here, I've had a piece of luck this morning. I hope this'll pay for all your matches.' She pressed the coin into the small girl's hand. Ella's mouth gaped as wide as her eyes. She clasped the coin tightly. Her face was still wet with tears, but she stopped blubbering and managed a diffident smile. 'No, it's *two* pieces of luck, that's what I've had. Those charms of yours is powerful stuff, missus,' she said to the grandmother. 'I'll buy more from you next time I see you, for sure.'

'He was trying to run you down!' the grandmother said. 'He swerved deliberately across the road towards you. It were no accident.'

'No, missus, you're mistaken,' Mary said and glanced towards the road the hansom had turned on to.

'Am I? Then why didn't he stop?' Granny said. 'If no harm was done, he'd have stopped, wouldn't he? If only to see if you was all right.'

Mary hesitated. It *was* odd. He didn't stop. In her mind's eye, she could see how he'd whipped the horse, urging it to go faster. But she hadn't been looking when she crossed the road. There was always the risk of an accident. But he had crossed the traffic – why would he do that? Maybe he should have stopped to see if he'd done any damage. Yet, she had the distinct impression that at the very last moment, he had swerved out of her way.

Mary brushed the remaining snow from Ella's dress. She took out a handkerchief and wiped the girl's cheeks.

'How can I thank you, Ella? I mean, it ain't often I

get my life saved,' Mary said. 'Here, tell you what,' she smiled, 'You look like you could use a feeding and I know just the place where you can get one. You like ham and mushroom pie? If not, there's plenty of others to choose from. Come on, let's fill you up. It'll put meat on your bones. You as well, Granny. It's only around the corner in Baker Street and it'll be my treat. Archimedes Dibble's Pie Shop, the best pies in London. I should know,' she winked. 'It's the only place I'd ever go for a pie. You mark my words, they're the best. And if you don't believe me, hear what your mouth says after a few bites.'

'Would you like that, Ella?' her granny asked and the small girl nodded with a sniff.

'Cor! You ain't half reminding me of me when I was your age, Ella,' Mary said as they started along. She was holding the girl's hand and granny limped beside them.

'She's a little ruffian!' Granny said and gave Ella a playful nudge. A smile broke the small girl's lips.

'That's me,' Ella announced proudly.

As they walked towards Baker Street, Mary noticed Mr Boots across the road. This was the second time she had seen him that day; it couldn't be a coincidence. It was such an odd sight that she had to stop.

He was standing at the corner where the hansom had turned, looking at her, and he did not attempt to conceal his gaze. A shiver ran down her spine – it seemed as if he wanted her to know he was there. She recalled his words: '*You and your friend think you're clever, little girl?*'

In the shadows behind him, only just visible, she saw the scar-faced man from the market. Her heart caught in her throat. At that moment, a smile broke Mr Boots's lips. But it wasn't a nice smile. There was something decidedly unpleasant about it. Mary felt a tight knot in her stomach as she hurried away.

When she looked back, Mr Boots was still there, watching – but yet again, the scar-faced man had gone.

10

THE BOGEYMAN

Ella's salivating mouth dropped open, her stomach rumbled mightily. Lunch for her was probably a piece of bread with cheese, some fruit or a potato, but now her eyes feasted on Grandma Dibble's pork pie, with its thick golden crust, surrounded by buttery mashed potatoes and green beans and carrots and lavished with brown gravy. This must have been something Ella could only have ever dreamt about. It made Mary laugh. The look on the little girl's face was a simple pleasure in a strange day.

Next to the plate were a hunk of bread, a saucer of butter and a glass of milk. Ella glanced at Mary in total disbelief, as if to ask whether this sumptuous meal was really for her.

'Tuck in,' Mary said. 'Otherwise, your stomach will

think your throat's been cut. Come on. The food ain't gonna eat itself. And it's the least I can do for you.'

Ella ate like a ravenous shipwrecked sailor at a banquet. She did not say a word as her fork speared the food, and up it went, and in it went, and down it went as she swallowed. She was relentless. Before long, her plate was empty. She finished the milk with a sigh of contentment and sat back into her chair, her hands around her stomach. And then, in a quite unladylike fashion, she gave a loud burp. Her hands quickly came up to her mouth and she looked around in embarrassment.

A round of applause greeted her as she glowed crimson.

'Well, this won't need a washing,' Grandma Dibble said as she cleared up the plate Ella had swept clean to a polish with the bread. 'Will it, greedy guts?' and she patted the girl's stomach.

Throughout the meal, Grandpa Dibble had fussed over Mary, asking if she was all right. Mary brushed off the incident with the hansom, making a quip about ending up on her behind thrice in less than a day.

'I hope you're not planning to make it a habit,' Archie joked.

But despite her efforts to think other thoughts, the events of the accident played through her mind. She could vividly see the steaming horse, the wild driver, feel the wind as the carriage sped past and hear Ella's warning shouts. Was it deliberate, like Ella's granny had said? Mary had read reports in the newspapers of a spate of accidents. She had stepped out, without a glance to see if it was safe. Was it any wonder she had almost been run over? But then there was Mr Boots, looking at her in such an odd way with hostile eyes.

'You all right?' Archie whispered.

'I don't get it, Archie,' Mary whispered back. 'He's following me. Mr Boots, I mean. He was outside when I left this morning, and again later on. And last night, as well.'

'He was the one following you?'

'How else did he know where I would be?'

Archie considered the question and shrugged. 'Well, maybe he needed to know where you'd be – to pay you the back wages.'

'Back wages?' Mary said irritably. 'That doesn't make sense. Come on, Archie, he didn't have to do that, did he? How could I complain about any money owed? I'm meant to be a thief, remember!' She folded her arms and fixed her jaws firmly. 'Look, Archie, he'd not shaved. I'm sure he'd slept in his clothes. That's not the Mr Boots I know. There he was with Mr Grimwig's lawyer. And then I saw him again just after the accident. Now that can't all be a coincidence – especially today of all days.'

'You're imagining things, *Mrs Holmes.* I've warned

you about them Penny Dreadfuls before. What? You saying he had something to do with the accident?'

'I'm saying…' she pursed her lips, narrowed her eyes and took a deep breath. 'Oh! I don't know what I'm saying, Archie. But twice in one day?' She gave a small groan of frustration, unable to sort through her thoughts. 'I'm saying there's more going on here than meets the eye.'

She got up in a fit of pique to stand beside the door.

Sally Dibble whispered something to Ella and both girls got down from their chairs. They surreptitiously disappeared behind the counter and then into the depth of the shop. But not stealthily enough.

'We're going soon, Ella,' Granny shouted.

'All right, Gran,' Ella replied, her laughs coming from the foot of the stairs leading to the floor above.

'She's not gonna end up in the poorhouse, not my Ella,' Granny said. 'It ain't a life for anyone, Mrs Dibble. Her mum can't look after her properly. She loves her dearly, but with the gin, she can't manage it. But I can manage her, if Ella could be properly taken care of, the little ruffian!' The old woman gave a weary smile that was almost tearful.

It was a smile of worry. Mary understood it well enough: who would look after Ella when her granny's time came? The smile was not lost on Grandma Dibble, either, who told the woman of the household of a friend in need of a scullery maid and that she would talk to them. She wasn't speaking about the Grimwigs, where there was now a vacancy, but of Mrs Rose Grady, a rich elderly widow who lived in Holland Park. It always amazed Mary: for someone who seldom left the pie shop, Grandma Dibble seemed to know so many people.

Mary knew that Ella would miss her granny and mum. After all, didn't she? She remembered the Fortesques, the people whom she had first been in service to, with some horror. She had spent her nights crying, but the next day she would hide her red eyes, not wanting the young master to know how upset she was. If he did, he would be twice as nasty as before.

But she was determined that it wouldn't be the same hardship for Ella, because she at least would visit her. And judging by the drumming of feet and the giggling laughter from above, a firm friendship was beginning between Ella and Sally, too. It was a happy sound. Mary remembered playing chase with her brother, with their mum running after them. There were times when such memories flooded back. What caused them, she did not know, although today it was probably the pleasant noises coming from up above her.

She was a little dreamy with the memory when she heard the screams. Shrill and sharp, they penetrated the pie shop and she jumped. The customers' heads flew up, forks clanged onto plates and chairs scraped back. The next moment, everyone went quiet as if holding their breath.

Mary and Archie instantly sprang up as the screams erupted again. This time they were more dreadful than before. Running towards the shrieks, rushing to the back of the shop and up the stairs, Mary and Archie nearly collided with Sally and Ella coming the other way. The two girls flew down the stairs, their eyes wide with terror. In their haste, they were taking two stairs at a time in a tripping, stumbling rush.

'It's the Bogeyman! It's the Bogeyman!' they shouted together as Mary grabbed one and Archie the other. The girls struggled and kicked, their arms flailing as they anxiously fought to get free.

'What are you two going on about?' Mary said.

'It's the Bogeyman,' they repeated, glancing back in a wild panic towards Mary's room.

Mary and Archie looked at each other. Dropping the girls, they dashed upstairs. When she entered the room, Mary gave a loud moan. Her meagre possessions, such as they were, lay strewn all around and about.

'What the hell happened here?' Archie asked.

The bed had been overturned, the mattress lying half on and half off the base, the sheets pulled away. Even the pillows were hanging out from the cases. The drawers of her cupboard were open and the handful of her things had been flung on to the floor. Her few books were lying wherever they ended up – where someone had thrown them. The storage boxes that were at the back of the room were all broken into and the contents tipped out. The window was wide open and a blast of cold air blew in the fluttering curtains.

Sally and Ella gingerly poked their heads around the door, hiding as best as they could, holding on to each other. Their faces were as white as sheets and terror widened their eyes.

Mary stood quietly amongst the litter of her belongings. She stooped beside the window and ran her fingers across the slushy snow. Impressions of boot treads lay across the floorboards. Her eyes followed them as they vanished into dark, damp water stains further inside the room.

Mary glared and spun around. 'Someone's turned over my room,' she said.

Archie went to the window. He leant out and glanced right and left. Suddenly, he dashed away and clattered down the stairs towards the entrance of the shop.

11

A STRANGE BURGLARY

Sally and Ella edged back into the room. They glanced around nervously. Still afraid, they stood close to Mary and she took their hands.

'All right, you two,' she said, 'what was it you saw?'

'The Bogeyman,' they said together.

Mary gave a deep sigh, pushed the mattress back, sat on the bed and drew them closer.

'Tell me,' she said patiently.

'We heard a noise in your room, Mary,' Sally said.

'We thought it was you,' Ella said.

'And we came in–'

'But he was there –'

'–the Bogeyman,' they said together.

The girls glanced nervously around as if expecting to see him again.

'He had a huge scar all over his face–'

'–and big scary eyes–'

'–one was red–'

They nodded enthusiastically.

'And he was dirty and smelly–'

'–and was all in black–'

'–and big hands–'

'–an-an-and he had a knife–'

Mary's fingers began drumming against her knee – a habit she had when thinking. She gave each girl a careful look. They were afraid. She shook her head slowly and smiled reassuringly.

'Go on, you two,' she said. 'Bogeyman! Some bloomin' burglar is what you saw. And good for you for shouting. Well, there's not much we can do here except tidy up. You better get back down, Ella. Your gran will want to be leaving soon, I expect. Now, you look after yourself and I'll look out for you when I'm next up Oxford Street way.'

Ella looked disappointed, but put on a brave face. As the girls walked downstairs, Mary could hear them talking excitedly about what they had seen. She went and leant out of the window.

There were fresh footprints in the snow at the back of the house. They came along the alley behind the shop and went back again towards Baker Street. No doubt that was what Archie had seen. She knew the prints would disappear in the slush of the main road, and so would the burglar into the crowd. Archie would be lucky if he found him.

She noticed how the thief had entered the room: he had climbed in from the small bay roof that jutted out below the window. She saw his boot prints deep in the undisturbed snow on the tiles, noticing the imprint of the treads was the same as in the slush on the floorboards, now quickly turning into water stains.

She checked the catch on the window. There were fresh scratches on the bare metal. It was as she thought: it had been forced probably with the blade of a knife. It was an easy thing to do. She had done something similar once before, herself.

She turned back to the room and chewed her lips. Her restless eyes washed across the mess; her fingers tingled in nervous anticipation.

'Strange,' she murmured.

Her locket was there on the chest of drawers where she had left it. It was made of gold and worth something. Not much, but something. She picked it up and placed it in a pocket.

All the drawers of the chest were hanging open, everything had been taken out. Her purse was on the floor. She picked it up. It still contained all her money: three pounds, three shillings and a penny.

Across the floor were her books. They looked as if they had been flicked through – like her belongings – all rifled and spilled where the thief had hurriedly thrown them. Each of the storage boxes had been tipped up and emptied.

She closed the window and sat down and drummed her fingers on her knee again.

'Nothing's missing,' she whispered.

A few minutes later, Archie came back, panting. He shook his head in defeat, confirming Mary's suspicions. He told her the boot prints were clear in the alley, but once they reached the pavement they vanished into the brown slush of Baker Street, along with the burglar.

'You're right, though: this room's been turned over,' Archie said and Mary nodded.

'Nothing's missing, Archie,' she said quietly.

'At least that's a blessing. I'll nail the window shut later,' he said. 'It'll not happen again.'

'No, Archie. You don't understand. *Nothing* is missing. Not from my purse,' she showed him the money. 'My gold locket was over there,' she pointed to where it was. 'All my books – they're worth a bit in a pawnshop. Even Grandpa's provisions,' she glanced at the open boxes. 'There was lots to steal – but *nothing* is missing.'

Archie looked puzzled.

'He didn't steal those things because he was looking for something else,' Mary concluded. 'He's no common thief. What have I got that someone could want, Archie?'

They went around picking things up, returning the room to the way it was.

'You think it was this Davey character – searching for the gems he thinks you still have?' Archie asked.

'Oh, no!' Mary shook her head. 'Not him. I've seen who did this before.'

'What?'

Mary picked up her signed copy of the Sherlock Holmes book.

'The man Sossie and Ella described – their Bogeyman – it was the man I saw in Smithfield Market this morning. I saw him again just after my accident. He was with Mr Boots.' She gazed up at the ceiling as if seeing him there. 'Oh! It was him, all right. A scar. Funny red eye. Dark and dirty. There can't be two like him. It's been a queer old day, and that's for sure, with Mr Boots, the snipe, the hansom and now this.'

Mary chewed her lips in contemplation.

'Archie, I swear, the second time I saw Boots, he wanted me to know he was watching me.' She trembled at the thought. 'There's something going on I can't explain. I still can't help thinking about what Mrs Grimwig said – "*Where are they? Has your friend got them?*" – when it was plain to see that all her jewels was there.'

'She was probably in shock or something.'

'She was shocked all right, but at something else.

After that argument they had, she comes out looking like thunder, and he just lets me go? If he was that concerned about the *criminal classes* finding out he was nearly burgled, wouldn't it have been better to have me arrested, and then boast: "This is what happens when you try to rob a Grimwig"? Instead, he wants it all hushed up – "*Mum's the word,*" he says.'

She slumped on to the bed and gazed thoughtfully to the floor. Her brow had furrowed, her fingers again drummed her leg.

'What're you thinking?' Archie asked.

'It's like what Sherlock Holmes said about the dog in the night-time...' She held up the Sherlock Holmes book.

Archie looked puzzled.

'The dog didn't bark,' Mary said.

'So-oo, the dog didn't bark.'

'Don't you see, Archie? The dog should have barked. It wasn't what was there that upset Mrs G, but what wasn't there.' Mary stopped drumming her fingers and sat up. An idea glimmered behind her eyes. 'She expected to see something else when the jewels were tipped out, but it weren't there, and whatever it was, they think I've got it.'

'Then why didn't she just ask you for it?'

'Constable O'Connor is why.' Mary smiled broadly. 'They didn't want him to know anything was missing.

That's why Mr G went out of his way to say how everything was there.'

'Well, if it's something dodgy, it wouldn't surprise me. So, what was this thing that should have been there and wasn't?' Archie asked.

Mary shook her head. 'It can't have been more gems. It would have to be small and different enough for her to instantly recognise it when she saw it.'

'Small?'

'It had to fit into the bag that had the jewels.'

Archie nodded. 'So whatever this thing is, you think they tried to kill you for it?'

'Or scare me, more than likely,' Mary said and again her brow furrowed as her fingers began drumming once more. 'I'm the *brains!* That's what Mr G's snipe said.'

'Now you've lost me.'

'Mr G's snipe thought I was working with him – Emma's boyfriend, Davey. Together, we stole something as well as the jewels. The snipe said we got greedy – that was the gems he was talking about.' She sat back on her palms and closed her eyes and licked her lips thoughtfully, starting to understand what had happened. 'But Davey nicked something else that the Gs want back desperately. They thought I had it in the bag of jewels. Now they know for certain that I ain't got it, it means Davey must have it. I'm sure I'm right: they didn't arrest me because they expected me to lead them to him – and that's why Boots followed me. He thought I'd end up at Davey's door. Only I don't know Davey and came here instead.'

'I'm still lost,' Archie said. 'Tell me this, those jewels must be worth a fortune – hundreds, probably thousands. What could be more expensive than those?'

The jewels were expensive, yet Mr Grimwig barely seemed to pay them more than a cursory glance. She could see him now. He didn't even check to see that they *all* were all really there.

'Not what's more expensive, but what's worth more?' she mused.

'That's the same thing, ain't it?'

Mary shook her head.

'Whatever it is, Archie, I've got to find it before they do. Think about it: if Mr G gets back what he lost, then my freedom won't be worth tuppence. He can easily have me arrested for stealing his jewels. Which is what he'll do when he no longer needs me.'

'Maybe Dr Watson's friend will help you.'

'Mr Holmes? No. He only deals with important stuff. Not scullery maids accused of stealing. No, Archie, I've got to do this on me own.'

'Not on your own. I'm helping as well. I'm pretty good at finding stuff. So, where do we start?'

Mary sat quietly. She had read all of Sherlock Holmes's adventures, several detective investigations in various Penny Dreadfuls and a few other detective books. She was an avid reader of the *Police Gazette.* At the start of any investigations, facts were needed. Facts had to be chased down.

'Emma's boyfriend – Davey the thief,' Mary said. 'He would know what he took, since he took it. They'll be looking for him as well. I have to find him first.'

Archie nodded.

'I'm in the same boat as Mr Grimwig,' Mary said, 'except he knows what's been taken and I don't.' She sighed. 'And neither of us knows where His Royal Highness, Davey, is…' Mary gave a knowing smile. 'But they don't know that him and Emma were stepping out. She'll know where he lives. I've got one advantage they ain't: I've got Emma Watkins.'

12

EMMA WATKINS AND DAVEY TUPPER

After the midday rush, when the pie shop became quiet, Mary and Archie left to see Emma. A feeling she could not explain warned Mary that time was of the essence. The feeling said that if she did not move quickly, she could be left behind. She was happy to be finally doing something.

Before they left, she had asked Archie for some of his old clothes. Archie's clothes hung off her in an ungainly way, and she had to tie a string around her waist to keep the trousers up. Then, borrowing one of Grandpa's caps, she bunched her hair high and tucked it inside, pulling the cap lower to hide her face. She looked at herself in the mirror. As long as no one came near, she could easily pass as a boy. If Mr Boots or his friend was keeping an eye out for her, this way she might give them the slip. She could not take any chances.

Dot and Sossie gazed open mouth as Mary left her room and suppressing their giggles, followed her downstairs. Archie rolled his eyes when he saw her. As they began to leave she heard a tut from Grandma.

'I hope you and your friend won't be out too long, Archie,' she said. 'Even with Mary's help, I might need another pair of hands this evening. Grandpa's got some errands to run.'

At that, Dot and Sossie burst out laughing much to Grandma's surprise.

As they left, Mary glanced up to the windows of 221b and wondered about speaking to Mr Holmes. After all, she had little experience in criminal matters, and what was going on, she assumed, was less than legal.

She remembered seeing a tall, lean man with sharp piercing eyes and a hawk-like nose standing beside Dr Watson that day she stole the pie. She did not know then who he was, nor of his relationship with the doctor. Only later would she find out and learn about his remarkable exploits.

IT WAS ON ONE OF HER DAYS OFF FROM THE GRIMWIGS, when she was helping out in the pie shop, that she next saw him. Sherlock Holmes was with Dr Watson. Being hungry, they came into the pie shop for convenience.

The great detective looked particularly jaded. Mary remembered listening as he talked about some baffling case, fascinated by the tall gentleman's assessments, how one fact followed another until a long string of observations developed. He spoke simply and clearly until he stopped. His observations had run out, and he was quiet and lost in his considerations.

At that point, Mary said something. What she said and what prompted her, she could not recall. She immediately regretted it and felt embarrassed – she had dared to speak to a customer. But she had been so taken by the man's voice that she forgot herself.

To her horror, the tall gentleman turned sharply towards her. She could not read his expression, which seemed dark and foreboding, and his glower made her afraid. She was about to run back to the kitchen when he gave a short, sharp laugh.

'Ha! From the mouth of babes…' he had said, and then quietly murmured, 'Comes truth and wisdom, Watson.'

'What a remarkable observation, Holmes,' the doctor had agreed.

'Come, we must be off at once if we are to catch our man. The boat train departs from Charing Cross in less than half an hour; we shall find him there.'

'You know, then, who he is?'

'Indeed. We must hurry.'

The tall man rose and was just about to stride out of the shop when he stopped. He reached inside his waistcoat pocket, leant over and handed her a sovereign.

'Ad victorem spolias,' Sherlock Holmes said.

SHE'D NEVER FORGOTTEN THAT DAY. BUT THIS AFFAIR, she thought, would not be important enough for a man of his reputation. She glanced once more up to the windows of 221b, and then walked on.

On the way to the Grimwigs' house, Mary reiterated her thoughts in much the same way as Mr Holmes had spoken that day. But it was mainly for her own satisfaction; to make sure she had not missed anything. Her conclusion was that there were too many coincidences to be explained by mere chance. But one thing she could feel happy about: Emma's boyfriend's identity was still a secret to the Grimwigs.

Nevertheless, she was worried.

If Mr Grimwig discovered that the thief was Emma's boyfriend, surely the maid would lose her job. Emma may even find herself arrested as an accomplice. With that in mind, even disguised as she was, she knew she had to be cautious.

When they reached the house, Mary sent Archie to knock on the backdoor while she hid and waited behind a hedge on the street. It felt odd, to be so secretive in front of a house she knew so well. She had spent three years there. It had been her home. She had been in and out of it so often as to lose count. Now she felt like a thief, going back there again.

Emma and Archie hurried towards her. The maid was almost in tears when she recognised her friend. There was a dreadful atmosphere in the house, Emma reported. The mistress was raging mad at everyone, and she and the master had argued well into the early hours after Mary had left. The butler was just as angry. That she didn't understand – what had he to be angry about? After all, it was Mrs Grimwig's jewels that had been stolen. And to her utmost surprise, Mr Boots had had words with Mr Grimwig – a real rough and tumble, it seemed, that shook the house into quiet. Emma was no fool, she had kept her head down. She was always afraid of Mr Boots and pretended she'd not heard a thing. Even so, it was all very odd, Emma said, especially the way Mr Boots spoke to the Grimwigs.

'You'd think they were partners or something, Mary. He was very familiar. He kept going on about getting Bob involved, whoever he is. Mr Grimwig didn't want that, and they were at it hammer and tongs, they were.'

Something strange was going on. Mary had thought it

odd last night when she'd heard them arguing, now she knew it was odd. But why that was, for the moment, had to wait.

'I need to find Davey,' Mary said, quickly coming to the point.

'Everyone's looking for him,' Emma said. 'Mr Boots gave me an earful. I thought he knew about us, but thank God he didn't. He questioned everyone in the house, over and over again. I ain't never seen him so angry before.'

'Do they know who he is?' Mary asked.

'I didn't tell and no one else knows him – not even his name,' Emma said. 'But, honestly, I don't know where he is. We were meant to meet this morning, but he never turned up. I was going to have it out with him. God! I'm so sorry, Mary, for everything,' she sniffled.

'Now don't start all that blubbing.' Mary reached up and brushed Emma's hair away – the bruise had become an angry purple patch, and the maid flinched her head away, allowing her hair to drop back into place. 'Him, wasn't it?'

'He didn't mean it,' Emma mumbled and looked away in embarrassment.

Mary's eyes flicked upwards and she huffed. 'Look, Emma, it's like this. You ain't gonna like this, but here it is, nevertheless. Davey is a thief. He took Mrs G's jewels all right, but he also took something else. Whatever it is, Mr G thought I had it, and… and, well, a few things have happened because of that. No, don't ask – I'm still trying to make sense of it all. But I ain't got a clue what it was he took and I need to find him and get it back.'

'Where's he live?' Archie asked somewhat gruffly. 'And what's his full name?'

'Tupper. Davey Tupper. He's got lodgings in Whitechapel, in Hanbury Street. I been there once.'

'And how long have you known him?' Archie barked.

'Six weeks or so,' Emma said and glared at Archie. 'I didn't know he'd do something that stupid.' Her eyes dropped just as her hand started to rise towards her bruised face. 'He brought me flowers and took me to the theatre. He said he wanted to marry me, he did…'

'I bet he did,' Archie whispered, scornfully.

'Mary, why's he talking to me like that?' Emma said and pouted. 'We was planning it, we was. He said we'd get a position in the same household. Then we'd be together. I do miss him, Mary, even after what he's done… I know it don't make much sense, but I swear I didn't know he was a crook.'

'Tell me, Emma, did he always come to see you when the Gs and Mr Boots were away?' Mary asked.

'You know what it's like,' Emma blushed. 'I couldn't get away easily, so he had to come over to see me. I'd get the sack if the master knew I was seeing a man, so he came when they weren't there. The first time he came, cook was out – that's when you saw him, remember? Here, what are you getting at?'

'And he wanted to look around, I bet,' Mary said.

'To see how the other half lived, is what he said.'

'And I bet he took a good gander when he was there,' Archie said, sniffed and rolling his eyes.

'Well, I didn't see the harm,' Emma said angrily.

'Emma! Didn't it occur to you –' Mary huffed loudly, and became quiet and in control. 'Oh! It ain't your fault, Emma, none of this. He's a clever one, that's for sure,' and she frowned, more at herself than at the maid. 'Thank you for his address, we'll go and see if we can find him.'

Emma's eyes dropped low. 'Mary, thanks for not saying anything to Mr G about me and Davey. And what I said last night about you owing me… I didn't mean it; I was just scared and I'm sorry. I do know better – really. I was brought up to know to be grateful. Whatever I can do to make it up to you, I'll do, honest. But when you find him, will you tell him I really want to see him, Mary? Please. I feel such a fool…'

She looked down and sighed.

'Cheer up, Emma. You ain't no fool,' Mary said in a light-hearted way, but Emma still looked miserable. She gave the girl a hug and laughed. 'Oi! You tell that cat I'll be back for him, so he's not to get too comfortable now I'm not there.' A small smile broke Emma's lips. 'That's better, Watkins.'

They parted company.

Mary and Archie took the underground, catching a Metropolitan Line train from Baker Street heading east towards Aldgate and Whitechapel. Mary sat down heavily and placed her hand in her lap. It was a hot, uncomfortable, smoky journey that suited her mood.

'He used her,' Mary said and Archie nodded, 'to have a good looksee – what was where and where was what. Poor Emma – he didn't give a tinker's about her. Just wanted to rob the place.'

'She was his ticket in.' Archie sat back and folded his arms. 'He seems a bit free with his fists as well.'

Mary remembered the thief's raised hand, his frightful glare when they had bumped together in the snow and the bruise on her friend's face.

'Promises of marriage!' Archie scowled. 'She fell for that?'

'Why not? You don't know what it's like being a maid, Archie. If Mr Boots or Mr G knew she was stepping out with someone, she'd have got fired. She had to be secretive.'

'Which suited him down to the ground,' Archie said. 'Well, she'll be lucky if she sees him again, even if we do find him. I thought that at least would be obvious.'

'Not to Emma, it wasn't,' Mary said. 'When he knew where everything was, he must have come over on a pretext to see her and sneaked upstairs. The Gs was meant to be out last night, Archie. Boots as well. I bet he knew that. But they changed their plans because of the snow. Davey must have figured it'd be easy pickings, and he'd have plenty of time. He just chose the wrong day, didn't he?'

13
WHITECHAPEL

The light was fading quickly when they left Aldgate station. The day had not brightened and, in the afternoon, became quietly dark. The air was smoky with a fog that was creeping in from the river and filling the alleyways and passages. The streetlight would barely penetrate the gloom. Before fresh winds came to blow it away, it would become thick and yellow, evil and sulphurous. It was miserable, lowering-of-the-spirit kind of weather.

Mary was anxious to conclude their business, knowing that they would have to grope their way back if they tarried too long. The last place she wanted to be in such a fog was Whitechapel, even accompanied by Archie. Especially heading to Hanbury Street. That's where Annie Chapman – one of Jack's victims – had been found. Mary had read about it in an old newspaper.

Then afterwards, she'd read about all the others. Even though Jack hadn't been about for a time, his terrible presence haunted the area, he had not been caught and everyone feared his return.

The house on Hanbury Street was a soot-blackened brick terrace. Dark windows overlooked a dark street. Paint was peeling from the frames and the wood was rotten. The front stair to the house was made up of three steps, greasy with moisture.

The noise from a pub on the corner hummed and rose and fell in pitch, muffled by the gathering fog. Someone was playing a piano, and voices were raised in song. Two people were arguing not far from where Mary and Archie stood by the steps. Even so, they were vague shapes in the thickening gloom. A woman's voice shrieked and a man, his voice slurred and drunk, shouted abuse. A door slammed and it was just the man's voice they could hear in the mist, swearing and yelling to be let in.

Mary knocked several times on the door and waited. Someone shuffled up behind it. She could hear soft dragging footsteps creeping forward, trying to be as quiet as possible.

Eventually, a woman's sharp voice came from behind the door.

'Who's there?' she demanded.

'You don't know me, missus. I'm looking for someone that lives here.'

The door opened a crack and two world-weary eyes stared out, darting left and right. Seemingly satisfied, she opened the door wider.

A frail middle-aged woman, stalk thin with her housecoat pulled tightly around her, stood there. Behind her, the corridor was pitch black. The stale smells of unaired rooms and cooking drifted out from the house. The pale, sunken-faced woman glanced nervously to the sides, along the street and over their heads. She looked Mary up and down, but did not say anything, seemingly not curious about how she was dressed.

'Well?' she asked. 'What's it you want?'

'Thanks, missus,' Mary said. 'We've come to see Davey Tupper.'

'He ain't here.'

'But he lives here, don't he?'

The woman hesitated. Once again, she glanced all about her.

'Well? What if he does?' she said impatiently.

'We're his friends. He said for us to meet him here.'

The woman sneered and looked her up and down.

'He ain't got no friends. And when you see him, tell him he owes me two weeks' rent.'

She was about to close the door, but Archie placed a foot firmly inside.

'So where's he, then?' he asked, gruffly.

'Toast of the town, is he?' she said. 'I don't know

where he is,' and she tried to close the door again. But Archie placed his hand against it and it didn't budge.

She looked at the boy. Archie stood a head taller and was a good deal heavier than she was. Even though he was only sixteen, he could easily pass as older. She paused and became fearful.

'How many more of you are gonna be looking for him today?' she said, sharply.

'Someone else was asking for him?' Mary said.

The woman peered at Mary suspiciously. There was something deeply unpleasant in the thin-lipped sneer she constantly wore and did not try to hide.

'A gentleman came,' she said in a soft, leery way, lifting her head haughtily. 'He had his own carriage, he did. A proper gent, he was, with a proper silver cane, proper gentlemen's clothes and proper gentlemen's manners. Unlike your friend,' and she glared at Archie.

'And what did you tell him?' Mary asked.

'He gave me ten shillings for me troubles,' she said, smiled and slowly held out her hand.

'Come on, missus, do we look like we can afford ten bob?' Archie said.

'Nothing's for free – my time costs money.' She tried to close the door again. Archie's foot, though, remained steadfast, preventing it from shutting.

A change came to her pale face; the sneer became a vicious scowl. 'I don't like the looks of you two. You get your foot out of my door, or I'll shout for a copper. There's plenty around here since Jack's been about. Go on, get out, I ain't got anything to say anymore.'

'Come on, missus–'

'You get your foot out of my door. You hear me?' she snapped. Then she looked up and past Mary and Archie to an ill-dressed woman. As the boy removed his foot, she shouted, 'Who're you looking at, Lizzie Green?'

An ill-dressed woman, who did not pretend to be doing anything but watching them, stuck out her tongue.

'You, you old bat. Who else?' she snapped.

With Archie's foot no longer there, the old woman felt brave enough to swear under her breath, just loud enough so all could hear. Then she glowered at each one of them in turn, and especially at Lizzie Green. There was no love lost there. In a show of force, she slammed the door shut.

Lizzie Green, though, just jeered.

'Davey Tupper, you're wanting, is it?' she said. 'What's he done now?'

'He ain't done nothing,' Archie said. 'We're just his friends–'

Lizzie laughed. 'Ain't done nothing? That'll be a first. And she's right – he ain't got no friends, so you're none of them.'

'We just want to find him, is all,' Mary said.

'How much?' Archie asked with a sigh.

'Keep your money. What do you think I am?'

She took a step back, raised her head and shouted, 'Ten bob, was it, *Mrs Tupper?* Ten bob? Was that how much your gent gave you, *Mrs Tupper?* Not thirty? Bloomin' cheap, ten bob, *Mrs Tupper.'*

'Mrs Tupper?' Mary said.

'Davey's mum, who did you think she was?' Lizzie said and laughed loudly. 'Takes all sorts, son, don't it? So, he's got himself in hot water again, has he?'

'I guess you know what he's like,' Mary said.

'Better than you, I'll warrant.' Lizzie scowled. 'That bruiser will swing one day, that's for sure. And that gent who's looking for him is no gent and that's also for sure, no matter what he looked like. I'd happily place a bet on who'll get him first. A shilling'll get you ten – it's the gent ahead of the coppers. So, he's got himself in it, has he?' She sniggered as if taking pleasure in Davey Tupper's troubles. 'Well, I don't owe the sod anything. Try Bow. He has rooms down there with his wife and kiddie.'

'*Wife*?' Mary said.

Lizzie cackled when she saw the shock on Mary's face.

'Oh! Don't tell me. So, who's the poor dear this time with the wool over her eyes?' Lizzie smirked. 'Your mum, son? Your mum, is it? He's far too handsome for his own good. To think that old witch could have a son as pretty, you wouldn't credit it, would you?'

Lizzie started to walk away. She stopped, turned, and Mary thought she was about to shout again so Mrs Tupper could hear.

Instead, she said, 'Ask in The Crown on the High Street. They'll know where he's billeted. That's where he drinks these days. Too good for the likes of us, he is. But watch out for him, son. For all his prettiness, he's an evil so and so, and I wouldn't put murder past him. Your mum's best rid of him.'

She turned again and, before Mary could say thanks, Lizzie bellowed to a man across the street.

'Oi! Spencer, you old goat, buy us a drink, will you?'

Lizzie joined him, and they walked arm in arm towards the pub.

'Oh! Bloody hell, Emma,' Mary moaned as if the maid was beside her and not Archie. 'A married man, you stupid what's-it.'

'With a kiddie,' Archie reminded her.

'You shut up as well,' Mary snapped and Archie laughed. 'How am I going to tell Emma that?' She huffed, stamped her feet in annoyance and closed her eyes tightly. *Poor Emma,* she thought. How she had been used.

The noise from the pub rose briefly as the door opened. There was a sharp cheering, and then the noise fell away to a murmuring as the door closed again. They were alone on the street.

When she opened her eyes, Mary grimaced. The fog had thickened. She pulled her jacket closer. Feeling the iciness gripping her tightly, she turned quickly and stomped towards the Mile End Road.

'Come on,' she said. 'Let's get off to Bow. The quicker I'm out of Whitechapel, the better. And I thought we'd have a start on Mr Grimwig. A gent with a silver cane? That's his lawyer I met this morning.'

Archie reached out his arm and stopped her walking away.

'We're not going to Bow tonight, Mary,' he said. 'We'll make a fresh start tomorrow when it's light.'

'But she's probably told him where her son lives.'

'Don't be daft. She might have told him something, but it won't be where her son lives. There's money there. She'll keep him dangling as long as she can. She probably told him someplace he's been, but not where he is. She's not that stupid.' Archie shook his head. 'No, we'll track him down tomorrow. You need to simmer down. Come on, let's get home. If this fog gets thicker, we'll be playing Blind Man's Buff with Jack before long.'

Mary looked around. She could still make out the houses across the street. Perhaps it was her imagination, she could not decide, but the feeling of being followed was a constant presence ever since her realisation that Mr

Boots had done just that. And now her mind seemed to be playing tricks. Seeing vague and indistinct forms in the mist, she became nervous. A shadow she thought was trailing her would suddenly come closer and walk away, while others seemed to hang back. Someone screamed out in the fog from a distant street and she thought it came from where they had just walked. She imagined a thousand eyes spying on her and she looked around apprehensively.

Glad that Archie was next to her, she smiled at him. But a feeling of unease had taken hold. A sense of foreboding returned; time was not on her side. Things were happening too quickly.

'No, Archie, I'm going to Bow,' Mary said decisively. 'I know what you said, but I need to find him and it won't wait till tomorrow. It's what Mr Holmes would do – strike while the iron's hot. You can go back if you want, but I'm going on.'

'Don't be daft,' Archie said. 'I ain't leaving you alone for a minute in this soup. If you go to Bow, I go to Bow. But–'

'Thanks, Archie,' Mary said quickly and with relief. She felt braver now he was staying with her; she did not need to tell him how grateful she was.

When they reached the main road, the traffic was reassuring; the lights from the hansom cabs were pale yellow patches. In the misty gloom, the illumination from the shop windows seemed to flare. On the street corner, the chestnut seller's stove glowed like a red-hot pool. People hurried along, hunched up against the cold, their mouths and faces muffled in scarves.

Lady Mary Finch placed her gun away. She had just survived the murderous intent of the Witch Woman of Whitechapel. But she had the information she needed... cleverly prised out...

Damn! Mary said to herself. She couldn't concentrate. *Poor Emma* she thought.

14
A TRIP TO BOW

It was a cold walk along the Mile End Road. The gloom did not clear and the sulphurous smell of the fog hung thickly in the air. The road was greasy with ice and occasionally they slipped with a skid. But Mary's mind cleared and her fear lifted like always now that she was doing something.

Before long, they approached the public house. The Crown stood sandwiched between two tenements, the ornate building residing beneath two floors of boarding rooms whose dark windows overlooked the street. The windows of the pub were ablaze with light and shouts of laughter resounded from within. A bright-faced old man, his sleeves rolled up, was standing outside as if taking some time by himself. He was smoking and whistling, and his occasional singing competed with the noise from the pub.

The King of Spain's daughter...

Came to visit me...

And all was because of my little nut tree.

I skipped over water, I danced over sea...

His melodious tenor voice made the people walking past smile. They nodded their heads in appreciation and, after exchanging swift greetings, he carried on with his song.

And all the birds in the air couldn't catch me...

Mary watched him from across the road. Then she and Archie crossed over.

It turned out, he was the landlord of the Crown. He laughed knowingly when she asked about Davey. But he didn't enquire about their business. Instead, he gave them a wry smile. It was a smile of someone who understood, or guessed, that whatever their business might be, he didn't want to know. But it was clear he knew Davey well and the directions he gave led them towards Victoria Park.

'You watch yourselves,' he called out as they left, giving them a wink of his eye.

Before they reached the wide-open space of the park, they first had had to walk through crowded and densely inhabited streets, where miserable and dirty alleys led into dusty roads of dark tenement buildings. Two miserable grey rows of deeply unwelcoming houses, some boarded up, some crippled and held upright by wooden buttresses, some with dark windows, rolled back, mouldering away before them in a rutted street. An unwholesome smell mingled with the fog in the air. Newspapers, rubbish and much more besides littered the ground. In and amongst this detritus, emaciated rats scurried, sniffing and snuffing, eking whatever sustenance they could find.

This is a long way from the Grimwigs' splendid residence, Mary reflected, *on its wide well-kept avenues, and the sweep of Regent's Park with its magnificent trees. That is another world.*

She could not help but wonder, when she ran away from the Fortesques, would this dark street be the kind of place that would have claimed her, if she hadn't met, by God's good grace, the Dibbles? She could easily see her image in the sullen faces of the squalid children playing in the street; she saw how suspiciously they viewed her and Archie, and how quickly they summed up the two visitors – well dressed, but not so well dressed as to be too far above them. And since they did not look like anyone in authority, the children carried on playing, but always watching, always weary. Mary knocked on the door of number fifteen and waited.

A woman answered. She could have been in her early thirties, so Mary thought, but she looked considerably older. She also looked ill. Her face was dirty and puffed. She sniffled through her red nose and watched Mary with dark, morose eyes. Mary thought she saw blackened bruises on her face concealed by the fall of her hair and she remembered Lizzie and the innkeeper's caution. The woman had been pretty once, Mary observed. Now all the misery of life lived in those eyes. She looked worn down, with her dry cracked lips, and greasy hair and a bent, world-weary gait.

From behind her came the incessant cry of an infant. She did not invite them in, but stood clutching the door with bluish fingers.

'I'm looking for Davey Tupper,' Mary said and the woman gave her back a knowing look.

'What's he done now?' she asked.

Mary explained what had happened: the theft, how she had been blamed for it and how she needed to clear her name before Mr Grimwig changed his mind and had her arrested. She explained why she was dressed in trousers and jacket, like a boy, fearing she might be followed. She left out Emma's part, but she didn't need to, she realised afterwards – the woman had probably already guessed there would have been someone like Emma around.

'I ain't seen him for days,' the woman said, introducing herself as Katie Tupper. 'Not since last Monday. When he ain't here, he's usually at his mum's in Whitechapel. His loving mum!' she huffed caustically.

'We've been there,' Archie said. 'She's a piece of work!'

That made Katie smile and Mary briefly saw how pretty she still looked. 'Yeah, she's that all right.'

'I really need to find him, Katie,' Mary pleaded.

'He's got acquaintances all over the shop,' Katie said carefully. 'That's Davey for you. He could be anywhere. But his mum's the one he trusts. So, you worked for the Grimwigs?'

'My old employer,' Mary said.

'Nicked their jewels and couldn't keep hold of them,' Katie said. 'Typical. But I didn't think it were jewels he was after. At least not the way he was talking. There was something else he was to steal.'

'I sort of knew he wasn't after Mrs G's jewels, but not what he was really after,' Mary said.

Katie shook her head. 'Don't look at me. I don't know what that might be. He was hired to do a job at your employer's house some six weeks back. To nick something. The man who hired him needed his special talent, he said.'

Mary looked puzzled.

'His looks. His talk. The things I fell for,' Katie said sourly.

Mary understood.

'Why wouldn't it have been jewels?' Archie asked.

'He said the man that hired him told him there are

things worth more than diamonds. But Davey wouldn't tell me what that might be. "Guess," he says to me.' Katie sniffed in a snooty way. "How does someone with nothing get rich?" he asked me and taps his nose. I see now he was talking about your Mr Grimwig. "Well, it won't be because they're honest," I says. Davey just laughs. "Money buys diamonds. What buys money?" he asks me?'

Archie hunched his shoulders.

'It was a regular goldmine, he says,' Katie continued. 'He was spending the money before he had it. That's Davey all over. All he had to do when he got the stuff, he says, was to deal with the man who hired him. And I didn't think he meant doing business with him.'

The sound of the baby crying got louder, causing Katie to slip back inside leaving the door open.

'He's double-crossed his partner, that's what's happened!' Mary said. 'Whatever it is Davey stole, he wanted it for himself. Taking the jewels must have been sheer greed, just like the snipe said. At some point, he must have decided he could do better on his own.'

'That's a dangerous game. You don't want to cheat your partners.'

'Looks like he did. And now he's gone to ground.'

'What's she mean: *what buys money*?' Archie asked. 'Money buys money, don't it? Or am I missing something?'

Mary did not know.

After a minute Katie came back. She was clutching an infant, barely four months old, wrapped in a dirty shawl. The baby was pale and thin and bawling. She rocked him gently back and forth until he became quiet again.

'I had the impression that there was someone else in the game, another toff, as well as the one who hired him,' Katie carried on. 'But I don't know who he was. No doubt Davey has turned on him too, and wants it all for himself. It sounded as if he was playing with the big boys. They play dangerous, I told him, and he should leave well alone. But he never listens to me, does Davey.'

'Who's the toff that hired him?' Archie asked.

Katie pursed her lips. 'Some gent with a funny name. He paid him far too much, and upfront – not that I seen much of it.' The baby started to complain again. 'Come on, Timmy, go to sleep, please, won't you?'

Mary tweaked the baby's nose and he smiled back at her, his big blue-grey eyes sparkling. Katie's mouth curled in a smile as the baby gurgled.

'Poor little mite,' she whispered. 'Anyway, the toff has a big house. Davey went to it. He said it's the sort of place we'd have one day. As if?' She flicked her head around to the house behind her. 'Palace, ain't it? He's left you in it bad. I can see that. And now he's caught between the devil and the deep blue sea. If he clears your name, he'll dirty his – not that his is clean to start with – and it ain't like Davey to be so generous. I wish he'd stuck to honest pickpocketing instead of getting airs above his station.'

At that, Katie started back inside.

'Try his mum,' she added, 'He'll pitch up there.'

Mary sighed. Davey Tupper could be anywhere. She said thanks to Katie and pinched Timmy's nose again, causing the boy to giggle happily. Then Mary reached inside her pocket and pulled out her purse, and found a half-a-crown piece. She had forgotten the business card she had put in there and it tumbled out. Katie retrieved the card and Mary pressed the coin into her hand.

'For Timmy,' she said.

'Thanks,' Katie said. Her eyes looked down as if she was ashamed. 'Davey gave me a little, but every bit helps. Eh! Timmy, go on, say thanks to the *handsome lad*.' The baby just giggled when Mary tickled his feet. 'Eh! Milverton!' Katie said, reading the card. 'That's him, the toff who hired Davey. Milverton!' She gave the card back. 'I knew he had a funny name. Lives in Hampstead, lucky beggar.'

'Mr Grimwig's snipe?'

'Snipe? He's no lawyer, luv, that's for sure.' Katie laughed. 'Especially if he hired Davey to thieve from your Mr Grimwig.'

For a moment, Mary's mind was a blank. Then she shook her head in annoyance. Why did she think Milverton was a lawyer? It was because of the way he was dressed, his carriage, his manner, how he seemed to know Mr Boots and, she assumed, the way Mr Boots seemed to know him. But now she wondered about the two. They knew each other, all right, but not how she'd thought. She felt foolish at her mistake.

Then she remembered what Mrs Tupper had said about the man who visited her.

'Milverton went and saw Mrs Tupper, so you might get a visit from him soon,' Mary warned Katie. Then she added as an afterthought, 'He'll pay cash for information,' and felt embarrassed to have said that.

As they left and started walking back towards Bow, Mary's mind returned to poor Katie. Two and six would buy Timmy some milk at least. But if no one helped her out, she'd be in the poorhouse before long. Mary was grateful Archie didn't say anything; he would have said she was throwing good money after bad. She could almost hear his thoughts. But how could she not have helped? She knew he too had seen the bruises on the sides of Katie Tupper's face.

But there was a nagging feeling that Katie knew more than she was telling, a feeling that Mary could not shift. Perhaps she was afraid of her husband. Or perhaps she was just loyal. But Davey Tupper's trail had gone cold like the foggy air surrounding her. Mary was at a loss.

'I thought Milverton was Mr G's lawyer,' she moaned.

She took out the card to read the inscription.

Charles Augustus Milverton,

Appledore Towers, Hampstead.

Agent.

'Agent? Agent for what?' she snapped and stood deep in thought. Then she glared. 'Mary Finch! Stupid Mary Finch, you've got cotton wool for brains! Don't you ever listen? Oh, rot! Mr Holmes would never assume; he would have found out, and what did I do? I assumed and didn't listen. So much for being a detective.'

A puzzled but amused Archie looked at her as she continued to tell herself off.

'His words were: "*He's played us,*" and "*It's not nice being made a fool of.*" And something about keeping one's eyes on the prize.'

'Whose words?'

'Milverton's. When we met, he thought I was working with Davey, while Davey was working for him,' she moaned loudly. '*His* plan was to steal this *prize* he was on about. But that got messed up when Davey took the jewels as well.

'And played him for a fool?'

'He thinks Davey double-crossed me, just like he did

him,' Mary said. 'That's why he went to see Mrs Tupper – to find him.'

'Let me get this right,' Archie said. 'This Milverton planned the robbery, and Davey Tupper has taken the loot and legged it. Milverton's not a lawyer; so what is he?'

Mary shook her head. 'Now there's four people after Davey.'

Archie glanced over.

'Four?'

'Me, Mr G and Milverton. And that other person Katie mentioned, that other toff.'

'Then he crossed him as well?' Archie asked.

Mary gave a look that said, '*What do you think*?' She shook her head in annoyance, remembering what Mr Boots said: '*This changes things*'. It was her meeting with Milverton. That's what changed things, she knew that now.

15

DORIAN JANKES

It had gone seven in the evening. The day had darkened with the fog and the approaching night. They walked in silence. Mary's spirit was down and as gloomy as the air around her. Archie, not knowing how to help, remained quiet.

As they walked past Whitechapel and the Guildhall, turning down towards St Paul's before reaching Fleet Street, Mary considered her next move. She had misinterpreted Milverton's intentions. How odd, she thought, that such a well-dressed seemingly good-mannered man should be a criminal and hire Davey Tupper to steal. But to steal what? What was it Milverton said? Davey Tupper was in the wind! Where in the wind? She must hurry to find him – but where to start?

The sense of nervousness she'd felt when she'd seen

Mr Boots with the scar-faced man had not left her. As they walked towards home, every now and then, Mary turned to look around through nervous, edgy eyes. She could see very little in the foggy gloom.

'What is it?' Archie asked after she had done this several times. Mary looked at him sheepishly.

'Mr Boots. I keep thinking he's following me.'

'You're seeing ghosts,' Archie said. 'Anyway, he'd be looking for a girl and there ain't one here, is there?'

Mary did not reply. But she looked again. The fog, though, hid too many shadows and muffled any sounds. If he was following, she might never see him. She was glad to arrive in Baker Street after the long walk. She was tired, hungry and her feet were cold. It had been a long day and she was looking forward to some food and rest, a moment's peace to think again.

She saw the familiar sign, Archimedes Dibble's Pie Shop, and inhaled the delicious smells of baking. Her stomach rumbled in anticipation.

An elegantly dressed, pinched-faced gentleman gave a slight nod and passed a coin to a small boy beside him near the shop door. The boy was pointing towards her. She watched the man with curiosity as he came nearer. He walked with a heavy limp and used a cane for support. Lifting his hat, he gave a slight but polite and respectful bow.

Before Mary could say anything, he said, 'The boy's not mistaken? You are Miss Mary Finch?' He hesitated for a moment, surveying her carefully and how she was dressed.

He displayed the same fawning courtesy of someone she'd met only that morning. She was about to deny it, but instead she sighed in resignation. She looked him up and down, and then looked across to Archie, who was doing the same.

'You're not a snipe, are you?' she said curtly, not wanting to make the same mistake she had with Milverton.

'Snipe?' The gentleman was puzzled.

'Lawyer,' Archie said sharply.

'Lawyer? No, not a… *snipe.*' He smiled in his polite way.

'So, what is it you want?' Mary said.

'Walk with me and I shall tell you.' He turned towards Regent's Park.

'All right,' said Archie.

'No. Just Miss Finch, young man.' He lightly placed a hand on Archie's shoulder and smiled again. Opening the palm of his other hand to indicate the way, with a slight tilt of his head, he invited Mary to go with him.

Mary looked around. Even though it was evening, the streets were still crowded. However, there were no snorting horses about to bear down on her or dark shifty men with scars, watching with menace in their eyes. She felt she was in no danger, even if Mr Boots was spying on her from a shadowy corner, she could at least pass as a boy, dressed as she was and may not be recognised.

Nevertheless, there was something serpentine about the man's smile; it was disingenuously pleasant. His whole manner was careful but false. Mary shivered, suddenly feeling afraid.

They went only to the top of Baker Street. In the Marylebone Road, a coachman, dressed in funeral black with a top hat and crop, sat atop a dark glossy gold-trimmed carriage, complete with a richly decorated coat of arms emblazoned on the door. The blinds of the carriage were firmly drawn. Mary stopped not wanting to get nearer. The gentleman stopped also.

'I have a proposition,' he said. 'If you would kindly return the items you stole, you would be very well compensated. Money,' and he nodded towards the carriage, 'is not an issue. Perhaps you could name your price.'

Mary was exasperated. She was getting tired of having to explain herself, and now she had to do it again.

'How many times have I got to say it? I don't know anything about whatever it is you want.'

'Come, come. Coy is one thing, but must we bargain?' He talked as if he was bored and had something better to do, but because of this tedious duty, he could not. 'We are not seeking a negotiation, Miss Finch. You are a thief, that is a fact. You were found with Grimwig's jewels, that also is a fact. Your greed is obvious. You took what you wanted, then you took more than you needed – that is yet another fact. We have been informed that the jewels have been returned. My client wants the rest. Simply name your price.'

'I'm not bargaining. I didn't steal Mrs Grimwig's jewels, and *that's a fact,* so I just don't know what it is you want.'

'The items, of course.' He smiled his snake-like smile again.

'And they are?'

'Is this discussion necessary? You stole them, we want them. It is as simple as that. Name your price. One hundred? Two hundred? Three? Tell me and we can be done.'

Mary's mouth opened in disbelief.

'If you do not have them then your accomplice has. Tell me where I can find him and we shall offer him the same contract. But really, Miss Finch, games are not necessary.'

'Three hundred? Pounds?'

'Pounds. Guineas. Does it matter?' He seemed to look through and past Mary, as if to say how tedious the discussion had become.

'Mister, that's more money than I can imagine. But I really don't know what you're talking about. If you tell me what it is you want, I might be able to help.'

The gentleman took a step back. He glanced at the carriage, and then turned once again to Mary.

'My client has not given me that information, only that you would know the content of our discussion,' he said coyly, and then angrily, 'But I fail to understand your reticence. He is prepared to offer what you ask. If you need to consult your accomplice, by all means, do. Agree a price with him, but be quick. Be careful, Miss Finch. The game you are playing is a dangerous one and could easily get you hurt, or worse.'

Mary scowled indignantly. The gentleman continued regardless.

'You have been keeping bad company, if I may say so. My client is aware of your meeting with Milverton. Understand well, my client's patience is limited. He is also dangerous and will get his way in this matter. Should the items not be returned, or should they fall into the wrong hands, he will seek recourse, of that you can be certain.'

Anger burned in Mary's breast. She was tired and annoyed. It seemed futile to protest. He would not believe her, she realised, no matter what she said.

'My card. You may contact me when you have made a decision.'

The card simply gave a name, Dorian Jankes, and an address. The gentleman tipped his hat. Mr Jankes took several steps. He stopped and turned back.

'Tell me, Miss Finch. Does the name Davey Tupper mean anything to you?' He kept his eyes fixed on hers as if searching for clues in any answer she might give.

Mary's eyes flickered for a moment. He did not press the matter further – he smiled politely once more, turned and walked across the road, and climbed into the carriage that moved away down Baker Street.

She turned and walked back to the pie shop.

'What was that about?' Archie asked.

'This is getting stranger by the minute,' she complained loudly. 'He offered me money for whatever was stolen. Three hundred guineas, if not more.'

'Three hundred!' Archie whistled.

'He asked me if I knew Davey. I think he guessed I did.'

'It's a tempting sum, Miss Finch. Three hundred guineas.' A lean, rather ferret-like man, sallow-faced with dark eyes, spoke to her. He was standing by the Dibble's doorway, acting like a customer, but his eyes were watching the elegant carriage make its way along Baker Street. A second later, Constable O'Connor exited the shop with a confident self-important swagger and stood by the gentleman.

‘Inspector Lestrade,’ the sallow-faced gentleman introduced himself and graciously tipped his hat.

Mary’s skin prickled.

‘Of Scotland Yard?’ she asked cautiously, already knowing the answer.

He nodded. ‘The same.’

16

INSPECTOR LESTRADE OF SCOTLAND YARD

She knew of him, Inspector Lestrade of Scotland Yard, because Dr Watson had mentioned him several times. She had even met him once some months back when she was witness to an incident in Greek Street. He had paid her little attention then. She knew him to be, in the doctor's words, *'The best of a bad lot'*: tenacious; a bulldog who lacked imagination, but was quick and energetic.

Mary also knew Lestrade had worked cases with Sherlock Holmes, and by all accounts – and here she could not reconcile Dr Watson's pronouncement regarding his lack of imagination – he had bested the great man on several occasions, or so the newspapers suggested. However, Dr Watson always spoke of Lestrade in a way that gave the impression he knew more about what had happened than the papers reported.

‘Will you be taking it?’ Lestrade asked. ‘It’s a tempting sum.’

‘I don’t know what you mean,’ Mary answered, but her voice sounded as if someone else was speaking.

Lestrade did not press her.

‘Perhaps, *Master Finch,* we should get out of the cold and this fog.’ He smiled and indicated to the door of the shop.

They went inside where Mary felt safe among the people she knew and trusted. Ignoring some of the strange stares she received, though she wondered if it was because how she was dressed or the company she was keeping, she and Lestrade sat in a corner. The inspector politely removed his hat, while Archie and Constable O’Connor stood and shielded them from the prying, inquisitive eyes of the customers. Dot and Sossie, understanding Mary was with a policeman, were watching Lestrade suspiciously and he beamed a smile at them in return. However, two dyspeptic faces continued to watch him unrelentingly.

‘Several curious things have happened, Miss Finch,’ Lestrade began. ‘If you’ll pardon me, aren’t you a little young to be a jewel thief?’ He immediately held up his hands as Mary was about to speak. ‘Constable O’Connor has been keeping me informed. Or perhaps it was the Davey you spoke of that did the robbery? By the by, who is he? Three hundred guineas,’ he ended absentmindedly.

Mary remained quiet and stared at him apprehensively. Lestrade shrugged.

'I cannot for the life of me understand why Mr Grimwig did not have you arrested. By all accounts, you were caught red-handed. Mr Grimwig, no doubt, has his reasons. There are rumours of a knighthood. So, perhaps *Sir* James did not want a scandal to mar such an auspicious occasion.

'I shall take you into my confidence, Miss Finch. It is common knowledge anyway. It is a practice to look into the affairs of some individuals who are about to be so honoured by Her Majesty, to see if they are of good character. You take my meaning? A knighthood is not a thing that is given lightly. My directive is to make sure that those receiving such an honour are deserving of it and beyond reproach. So you can imagine my concern when I was told of your little escapade last night by Constable O'Connor.'

Lestrade sat back and became comfortable.

'I know little of business, Miss Finch, so I can only guess at Mr Grimwig's success. Indeed, a success he has been. He has pulled himself up by his bootstraps, make no mistake about that. His success is, no doubt, a resounding testament to his industry. To date, I believe, he owns a cotton mill in Lancashire, the house on Regent's Park, he does business in the city, to name but a few of his concerns. He has a reputation as a charitable man. I think you would agree, having been the recipient of his benevolence. And, of course, he supports many fine causes – financially and morally. He has come a long way from such humble beginnings in Manchester to Regent's Park.'

Lestrade paused and Mary waited in silence.

'Such men are at risk from thieves and conmen and must constantly be on their guard,' Lestrade continued. 'The things people will do, Miss Finch, to embarrass them are too numerous to mention. And we at Scotland Yard are charged with making sure such events do not take place. This we do diligently, Miss Finch. Diligently.' He nodded. 'So, given all this, I was very dismayed to hear that you have been keeping company with one Charles Augustus Milverton.'

He said the name slowly and deliberately and looked at Mary to see if she would react. The scullery maid, however, sat stony-faced. For a second, it disconcerted Lestrade.

'You don't deny it?'

'I'm hardly keeping company with him, sir. I met him once only.'

'That we know of.'

'I thought he was Mr Grimwig's snipe when I met him.'

'A lawyer?' Lestrade's hand came up to cover his mouth and he gave a slight laugh. 'Come, come, Miss

Finch. Mr Milverton is as much a lawyer as you are… well, the Queen of Sheba. The only thing he knows of the law is how to use it to his advantage. He is a dangerous man, Miss Finch, and we at Scotland Yard know him for what he is. On several occasions, he has come to our attention. The man is a blackmailer. A very accomplished one. He's ruined many in his time. He makes it known that he would pay handsomely for information. And where does he get such information? From valets, butlers, maids – yes! even scullery maids.'

Mary's mind was racing now she'd found out who Milverton was. She was aware of just how intently Lestrade was watching her and she felt as if she was a specimen under a microscope. She struggled back to the present. Suddenly feeling hot, she hid her eyes.

'Pay, like… as much as three hundred pounds?' Mary asked.

'A niggardly sum, to be sure, if the information is genuine and damming – is your information so?' Lestrade smiled.

'I don't know what you mean,' Mary said.

'Think what you could do with such a sum were you to be tempted. Or have you been so already? I must warn you, Miss Finch. If it is your intention, or that of your accomplice – Davey, is it? – to sell to Milverton something you have stolen and thus embarrass Mr Grimwig, then be careful, as we are on to you. The law will not be kind, even taking into consideration your age. I can assure you of that.'

Again, he looked closely at Mary, while again she sat impassively. But her mind was elsewhere. Her fingers were drumming.

'There, I have said my bit. It is up to you to do rights by your former employer. We shall be keeping an eye on you, Miss Finch. Be sure of that. You will be in need of a *real* lawyer should you persist in following this foolish course.'

'Inspector, I know of your reputation with Mr Holmes and the great respect he has for you, so I won't lie.' She saw Lestrade perk up at the compliment. 'I didn't steal anything, despite what Constable O'Connor said. I know what it looked like, but I only picked up the gems when the man dropped them.'

'This… Davey?'

Mary nodded. 'But that's all I know. Mr Milverton approached me. I ain't never seen him before. I don't know who Davey is. I really don't know anything. But if you can find Davey, then I know things will get sorted out.'

'You were in the wrong place at the wrong time? Is that your contention?'

Mary gave a weary nod.

'Very well, Miss Finch, if you intend to persist with this charade.' Lestrade sighed. 'I believe last night Mr

Grimwig asked if you knew this man – this thief. You said, no. Now, by some magic, you know his name – Davey. Then Milverton, a noted blackmailer, approaches *you*, a lowly maid – you're hardly someone in whose society he would mix. Then another gentleman, well above your station, offers you three hundred guineas, and you say you don't know why he should do that. You see the problem I have, don't you?'

Mary sank deeper into her chair and her shoulders drooped. She wanted to argue, but her mind was as tired as her body.

Lestrade rose. He carefully slipped on his gloves and walked to the door where he tipped his hat and gave a slight nod and smile to Dot and Sossie, who were still on sentinel duty, fully armed with scowls. Constable O'Connor followed and glanced back, smirking.

'I must say, Miss Finch,' Lestrade said as he opened the door, 'you keep fine company. The Earl of Marshmere. It was he in the carriage, I take it?' and Lestrade nodded towards the direction of the Marylebone Road.

Mary followed his gaze and took a deep breath. She needed him to leave so she could think.

'Lions and Unicorns is his crest, after all. Dorian Jankes is his man. Though if the truth be told, Jankes only ever works for himself. He is not someone you would want to do business with, Miss Finch. You must trust me in this. His reputation is dubious, to say the least, and he is someone else known to us at the Yard. He is an opportunist. However, that aside, I think you will find troubling Mr Grimwig to be one thing, but a peer of the realm something quite different. I see I shall have to keep an eye on you, Miss Finch. A very close eye.'

17

MARY MAKES A PLAN

The visit from Lestrade disturbed her. Now Scotland Yard was involved, it meant that Mr Grimwig could no longer keep the affair a secret. She considered what Mr Grimwig would do if he could not retrieve his property. Would he throw her to the police through sheer spite? Despite all Lestrade had said about his charity, Grimwig had changed in her eyes, and such an action would not surprise her in the least.

And now there was yet another player involved: the Earl of Marshmere and his man, Dorian Jankes. *Was one of them the other gent, Katie mentioned?* she wondered. What had Davey Tupper to do with a peer of the realm? Or nobility with this affair?

She rose early on Sunday after another fitful sleep. The fog had lifted and the sun was out, and her careful examination of the events had resulted in what Mr

Holmes would have called a working theory. There was, nevertheless, something missing, and to fill in the gap, she would need to talk to her friend, Emma, and then visit the library tomorrow.

The Dibbles were all wearing their Sunday best, ready to attend church that morning. They all left when Dot and Sossie had found their hymnbooks, turning east and making their way to Grandma's favourite church, All Saint's in Margaret Street.

Walking some of the way with them, and dressed once again in Archie's old clothes, Mary surreptitiously glanced around until she was satisfied that no one was following her. Once they turned a corner with several streets nearby, she broke away and turned north towards Regent's Park. The Grimwigs always attended eight o'clock service with their staff, and Mary hoped to catch Emma at some point. She would still have to be careful, however, as she did not want either the Grimwigs or Mr Boots to see her.

Hidden by a screen of bushes, Mary watched the church party walk across the still snow-white park. She followed them at a safe distance and managed to catch Emma's eye just before she sat down in her pew at the back of the church. Mary flicked her head as if to say, *'Meet me after'*. Emma nodded.

At the end of the service, the Grimwigs walked to visit friends on the other side of the park as usual, and their staff wandered back in the opposite direction. Mr Boots went elsewhere on his own business. Mary caught up with Emma and they lingered a while by the church.

'He's married, you know,' Mary said. 'Davey Tupper. He's got a little one as well. I saw his wife and the little one yesterday.' Mary had been wondering how to break the news to Emma and, in the end, decided to be blunt. However, she wanted to kick herself when she saw the look on her friend's face.

The maid gaped in disbelief and Mary gave her a hug.

'I always thought it was too good to be true,' Emma mumbled through tight closed lips. 'I mean, look at me, Mary. I'm plain, aren't I? I'm no catch, am I? I never knew what he saw in me.'

'You ain't plain and you are a good catch.' Mary brushed some lint from the maid's shoulder. 'You're the most kind-hearted soul I know. But he wasn't the one for you, Emma, it's as simple as that, even if he wasn't married.' She ran her finger across the purple bruise.

Emma's spirit was low. She nodded her head in recognition of Mary's efforts. But her tears betrayed her disappointment, making it a hard task for Mary to explain how Davey had used her as a means to get inside the Grimwigs' house.

Emma was silent throughout Mary's account. She merely nodded or shook her head, depending on what was being said, but Mary could sense her hurt. When Emma did speak, her voice was cracked and broken.

'God! I feel such a fool, Mary. He kept asking me all sorts of questions about the Grimwigs. I just thought he was being polite. And all the time, he was making notes about how to rob the place. I was never that clever, Mary, was I? Not like you. But honestly, he made it sound so convincing – marrying, getting a position in the same place…' her voice fell away into sniffles.

'He's a flimflam, Emma. He could fool anybody. He's that good. But now you know, things'll be fine.'

'They won't. I mean, how am I gonna trust another bloke again?' She looked down despondently and grimaced. 'And what about you? None of this would've happened if I'd never met Davey Tupper. Yesterday I overheard Mr G talking about getting you arrested. And he meant it. Him and Boots were talking – arguing, if you want to know.'

The news did not surprise Mary. She had feared this and felt it would come before long.

'Who knows what would have happened, Emma?' Mary said and squeezed the maid's hand. 'Now, stop beating yourself up about it. Look, I need to know something. I met this copper yesterday, an Inspector Lestrade. Anyway, he was telling me about this gent called Milverton – have you heard of him?'

'Milverton. I met him a couple of months ago. He

gave me the shivers. A creepy bloke – and that smile of his–' Emma turned her nose up in disgust and Mary nodded in agreement. 'He stopped me in the street in front of the house, he did, and said he knows me. I was taken aback when he said that. I mean, how could he know me – me a maid and him a gent? Then he says he could give me enough money that I could set myself up in a nice teashop in Epsom or Brighton or somewhere. I could be my own boss with a maid of my own. Imagine that. Me! *Lady Watkins.*' She laughed.

'That sounds like the gent from what I know of him. So, what did he ask you to do?'

'Well, that's the thing, Mary, he never really told me, proper like. He asked if the Grimwigs knew the Earl of Marshmere.' Mary startled at the mention of the name. 'Then he gives me ten shillings – for my time, he said – and then… well, I didn't know why that was worth ten bob. It weren't no secret. I saw the Earl. Cook saw him as well, and Mr Boots, and the gardener and the footman, and God knows who else. I'm surprised you didn't.'

Mary shook her head. She had never seen the man.

'So, I told him. I mean, what was the harm? The Earl had come over to see the master once, and was he angry! He was shouting and screaming. I wasn't spying, Mary, it's just that the commotion could be heard all the way to the kitchen. I told Mr Boots he should call a copper, because it sounded as if someone was going to get brained. Did I get an earful about minding my own business! Anyway, when I told Mr Milverton, he burst out laughing.'

Emma twisted her head sideways, her brows furrowed.

'That was a bit queer; I mean, I didn't see the joke. When he finally stopped laughing, he said there are some items, probably in a drawer or box in the Gs' bedroom he's interested in. They really should be in a safe, he says, but he knows Mrs G and she'd have them near her. Would I be interested in getting them for him? Then he'd pay me for my troubles – much more than ten shillings.'

'What were they, Emma?'

'He never told me, just wanted to know if I were interested.'

Mary sighed loudly.

'He says to me no one would know if I took them except him and me, because the Gs wouldn't do a thing about it. But he needed to trust me first, he says. Mary! He wanted me to steal from Mr Grimwig. I was honest shocked.' Emma screwed up her lips in annoyance and became louder and more animated. 'I'm not that sort of girl. I wasn't going to steal from the Gs, no matter what he was going to pay me – teashop in Epson or what. And I told him straight, I did. I even gave him back his ten shillings. He told me, all la-di-da like, to keep it and think about it, and that it was just a business proposition. He gave me his card, he did. He said I should come and see him when I changed my mind. But I threw it in the gutter in front of him, I was so disgusted.'

Emma stood with her hands on her hips and pouted angrily. Mary had never seen her friend so worked up before, and when she laughed at the sight, she saw a smile break Emma's face.

'And that was it, Mary. I never saw him again.'

'I'm proud of you, *Lady Watkins.* But then you met Davey a couple of weeks later?' Mary already knew the answer. She saw the smile vanish.

'He comes up to me in the park on me day off, and says he's been watching me and how pretty I am. Well, I am pretty sometimes.' Emma blushed. 'Anyway, he says, "Why don't we walk out?" Well, you know, I mean, it was a bit forward, but he was handsome, very handsome, and… and… well! You know!'

'Wined and dined you, did he?' Mary nudged her. Emma laughed.

'Well, tea and cakes, anyway.'

'That's what I figured; I just had to be sure.'

'I'm ever so sorry for all the trouble, honest I am.' Emma looked down at the ground. 'We're still friends, aren't we, Mary?'

'Shame on you, Watkins!' Mary feigned anger. 'We were never anything else. What's done is done. Oi! By the way, how's Oscar?'

'Misses you, he does. He's even taken to doing some work, he misses you so much. He caught a mouse yesterday, in the pantry. Didn't know what to do with it, though. I had to knock it on its head for him because cook wouldn't.'

'Daft cat! Tell him I'll be back for him. And you take care, Emma.' Mary grasped the maid's hand tightly and leant closer to her. 'And don't – you hear me, Emma Watkins – you *don't* tell Mr Boots or the Gs about Milverton. You've never met him, you don't know who he is. You've never even heard his name before. He's trouble. And if they ask about the Earl of Marshmere, it wasn't you that spoke to anyone about him.'

'I might be daft, Mary, but I'm not stupid as well.'

'Good on you. Now, I've got to go.'

What Mary had suspected was true. Some details she was still unsure of, but she was beginning to understand the chain of events. She was playing through a plan. The next step was to see Mrs Tupper again, now she knew what questions to ask.

As she walked she lost track of time. It was mid-afternoon when she turned into Baker Street. The sky had clouded over and darkened, and in the heavy gloom, an early evening threatened. Mary noticed the lights in the windows of 221B were burning brightly, and again she thought about knocking on the door and speaking to Mr

Holmes. She could put forward her theory and see what he thought.

She imagined him, eyes closed, pipe in hand, carefully examining her words, and then agreeing – just the way he did that day in the pie shop. At that point, the chase would be on.

Mary shook her head solemnly. No doubt he would be involved with bigger game and her concerns were small in comparison. Then her stomach rumbled and the lights in Archimedes Dibble's Pie Shop burned so much more brightly than Sherlock Holmes's with the promise of food.

Nevertheless, her mind was clear. Tomorrow, with Archie's help, she would follow through with her plan and go and see Mrs Tupper.

18

A MURDER IN WHITECHAPEL

'Murder! Murder in Whitechapel! Has the Ripper struck again? Murder! Woman found dead in Whitechapel! Is the Ripper back?'

The paperboy bellowed across the street from the pie shop, doing brisk business. Archie rushed out and returned with Monday's early morning edition.

BRUTAL MURDER IN WHITECHAPEL, THE headline screamed.

SECOND DEATH IN HANBURY STREET.

POLICE SUSPECT THE RIPPER.

Archie read aloud from the newspaper as Sossie and Dot sat open-mouthed, listening.

A most brutal murder was committed in the neigh-

bourhood of Whitechapel in the early hours of yesterday morning, but by whom and with what motive is at present a mystery.

At a quarter past four o'clock, Police Constable Bennett, 83J, when in Hanbury Street, Whitechapel, came upon the body of a woman lying in the front door of a house, and on stooping to raise her, in the belief that she was intoxicated, he discovered that she had been murdered.

A message was immediately sent to the station and for a doctor. Dr Staples of Whitechapel Road, whose surgery is not a quarter of a mile from the spot where the woman lay, was aroused and proceeded at once to the scene.

Doctor Staples made the following statement:

'I was called to Hanbury Street about five minutes past five this morning by Police Constable Bennett, who said a woman had been murdered.

'I went to the place at once and found the deceased lying half in and half out of a house in Hanbury Street. She was lying on her back with her legs out straight, as though she had been laid down. I was assured that the body had not been touched.

'On feeling the extremities of the body, I found that they were still warm, showing that death had not long ensued.

'A crowd was now gathering, and it was undesirable to make a further examination in the street.'

After the body was removed to the mortuary of the parish in Old Montague Street, Whitechapel, steps were taken, if possible, to identify the victim.

A woman answering the description of the deceased was the owner of a common lodging house in Hanbury Street, Whitechapel, where the body was found.

Lodgers from that place were fetched, and they identified the deceased as she from whom they had rented rooms at a nightly payment of 4d each. Elizabeth Green, at present a resident of Whitechapel, was also taken to the mortuary and identified the body as that of Mrs Virginia Tupper.

FOR A FEW MINUTES, MARY AND ARCHIE SAT IN SILENCE while Dot and Sossie whispered energetically. Mary read the article again. There was no mistake: Mrs Tupper, Davey's mother, had been murdered.

'What're you thinking?' Archie asked.

Mary remained quiet. Her mind raced. The plan had been to go and see Mrs Tupper that very day and plead with her, somehow convince her to help. Now she was at a loss.

'We only saw her Saturday,' Archie said. 'Should we tell the coppers? Why would Jack want to murder her?'

'The police? I don't want to see them, Archie – I'm in enough bother as it is and I don't like the looks of that Lestrade. And it wasn't Jack who did this. He cuts his victims up, he doesn't strangle them, so it ain't him. They're just trying to sell newspapers saying it was him – especially seeing as where it happened. Anyway, she's not the kind of woman Jack preys on. The coppers will know that.'

'Then who'd want to kill her?'

'I can think of a few,' Mary said. 'Milverton. Mr G. Maybe even that Earl. Or someone else – a robber, maybe. No, this has something to do with her son. I'd wager she knew where Davey was and whoever did her in was trying to get her to tell. It's too much of a coincidence. They're sending a message to Davey Tupper.'

'*Give up what you took or else!* I just had a thought,' Archie said. 'Lizzie Green. She saw us.'

'I know, but it was two lads she saw, remember? Not a boy and girl. I think she'll tell the police about the man with the cane – they may even find Milverton's card in Mrs Tupper's house, not that it'll prove anything. But Lizzie won't tell about us, I'm pretty certain of that. It's Katie and the kiddie I'm worried about. Whoever killed Mrs Tupper will be looking for Katie if they find out Davey was married. But who knows what Mrs Tupper might have said before she was killed?'

Mary gazed out of the window. The newspaper boy

had almost sold out. The feeling that time was running out returned. She felt a sudden chill and shivered.

'Then there's me, isn't there, Archie?' she said quietly. 'They still think Davey and me planned this. Milverton thinks that, and the Gs. Jankes and that bloomin' Earl as well.' Mary's finger drummed against the table. 'The only thing I've got going for me is that they think Davey's cut me out and gone into business on his own. It'll help if they think he cheated me – they might leave me alone. Davey Tupper's bitten off more than he can chew. All right, he's got the goods, but now what does he do with them? He's a pickpocket, a conman, and this is all about blackmail.'

'Blackmail? How do you figure that?'

Mary sat back and thought for a few seconds, recalling some events.

'It's the only thing that makes sense, Archie. Lestrade said that's what Milverton is about. I know he hired Davey to steal from Mr G. I know it wasn't about jewels. If it were, Mr G would have had me arrested then and there. The only reason I'm free is that Mr G thought I knew Davey's whereabouts. But what I don't get is the Earl. I mean, who was Milverton planning to blackmail?'

'Grimwig! He was the one that Davey nicked from.'

'I get that. But the Earl was willing to pay a fortune for the *items.* And if one of them killed Davey's mum, then that changes things, doesn't it? The stakes are much higher all of a sudden – I mean, you hang for that sort of thing.'

'I hadn't thought of that,' Archie said.

'Katie was right, Davey should have stuck to pick-pocketing. That's more his game.'

'I guess he thought it'd be pretty easy money. But how do you do it? Where do you start with blackmail?'

'By being clever, that's for sure,' Mary said. 'You need some brains for that – and I'm coming around to thinking that Davey Tupper hasn't got any. I mean, he even used his own name when he courted Emma.'

Mary pushed her chair back and stood gazing out of the window.

'He might be able to blackmail the people he normally mixes with and a few others who don't know better,' she said, 'but people like the Gs and the Earl are way beyond his understanding. That's why the toff lives in Hampstead and Davey in Bow. Milverton's behind all this. Now Davey's got something that's burning a hole in his pocket.'

Mary turned back towards Archie. She knew what she had to do and did not need to ask for his help.

'Listen, Archie, I've got to go and see Katie Tupper,' she said, 'and quick as well. I think she knows where Davey is, or has an idea anyways. I've got to warn her at least. Though she might guess when she hears the news about her mother-in-law. If they find out she and Davey are married, they'll be calling, and they won't be taking no for an answer.'

Archie stood up and folded the newspaper.

'The coppers will find her as easy as we did,' he said, 'and that was easy enough. The murderer will be able to do the same.'

They set out. This time, Mary did not bother with a disguise. With the death of Mrs Tupper, she wondered how effective it had been, but she did not tell Archie her thoughts. Having dropped Dot and Sossie by the school gate, they turned east and headed towards Bow. Mary said she needed to find something out about the Earl of Marshmere before they saw Katie Tupper.

'He's the piece of the puzzle I don't get,' she said and vanished inside a public library on their route. Archie followed, took one look at the books and announced his intention to wait outside.

Mary found what she needed between the covers of both *Debrett's* and *Burke's Peerage*. They each listed the history, place in society, marriages and such of all the Peers of the United Kingdom of Great Britain and Ireland. She was surprised to learn that the title of Marshmere came not from the Earl, since he was a commoner, but from his wife. She sat for a minute and reread the notations to confirm her suspicions, her fingers drumming the table.

Stepping back into the cold, she met Archie. Together

they started out again. Mary took a long look around her, noting who was about, fearing they might be followed. Every few minutes, she glanced back.

But something else worried her. She tried to sort her thoughts as they walked, but each time her mind wandered back to the meeting with Mrs Tupper. She felt sorry for her. Virginia Tupper had been an awful, grasping lady – Mary remembered how she'd held out her hand for payment when asked for her son's whereabouts. But then she was no more grasping than many, and for the same reasons as they. You have to live, after all.

As they hurried along, Mary's mind returned to Davey Tupper. Theft had turned to murder. Was murder something Davey ever considered? Then she remembered the bruises on Emma and Katie's faces and the coldness in his eyes that night.

19

KATIE TUPPER HAS VISITORS

The news of her mother-in-law's murder had already reached Katie Tupper. However, it had not arrived via the police, or by some kind soul who sought to ease her pain and inform her gently. That was clear to Mary, who had to knock for several minutes as a pair of dark eyes watched her nervously from a window.

When the door opened, Mary recoiled in shock and a wave of anger washed through her. Katie sported a black eye and several dark bruises. She raised her shawl to cover her head.

'Who did this, Katie?' Mary demanded, thinking her husband had returned.

'I never seen him before. An evil-looking man,' Katie whispered hoarsely.

'Let me in, I can fix you up a bit,' she said.

Katie shook her head, stood proudly erect and held the door firmly half-closed.

'Katie… it's Mrs Tupper–' Mary hesitated. 'I'm so sorry–' she stammered.

'I know,' Katie said. 'God forgive me, but she'll be no great loss. She and I never got on, and she didn't care tuppence for little Timmy.' A tear came into her eye that she hastily wiped away. Her face became rigid. 'But I wouldn't wish her to be murdered, and not because of a son who cares nothing for her.'

'You getting roughed up?' Mary asked. 'Was it because someone thought you knew something?'

'The bloke that did this wanted to know where Davey was hiding,' Katie said. She drew the shawl higher. 'He told me he'd killed her. He boasted about it. He told me how he strangled her and how she screamed. He described every bit of it. He was laughing all the time – the devil.'

She trembled at the horror. Mary understood – Mrs Tupper had not given her son away. Why else would her killer visit Katie?

'He said he'd do the same to me if I didn't tell him where Davey was. But I screamed before he could gag me. Then he gave me these,' and she raised her hand to her bruised face. 'But I just shouted and shouted and roused the whole house. When he saw what was happening, he ran, thank God!'

Mary reached out a hand towards her, but Katie pulled away, shaking her head.

'No one can help me,' she said. 'And I fear no one can help Davey either. You must think we're a right pair,' and she gave a sardonic smile.

Mary shook her head. Katie looked such a sad sight, like a frightened animal, hiding and wanting to be left alone to lick its wounds.

'I don't have the right to judge you, Katie, and I'd never do that,' she said.

Katie Tupper smiled kindly. 'Help yourself,' she said. 'Look out for that devil that killed her. He wasn't Jack like everyone's been saying, but he's just as evil, I'm sure. For as long as I live, I'll never forget that devil's face, that scar, that awful red eye–' Mary flinched in surprise. 'I'd have told him, then and there, if I knew. But for the life of me, I couldn't.'

She bit her lips and regained her composure, saying bitterly, 'So, this isn't just about stealing, is it?'

'It's more dangerous than that,' Mary said. 'Davey's trying to get into the blackmail game.'

'Is that what he meant about us being rich – blackmail?' Katie sniffed scornfully. 'He ain't got the brains to have thought that up himself.'

'That Mr Milverton put him up to it, I reckon.'

'Was it his man that did this?' Katie touched her bruises.

'No. I'm sure the man with the scar works for Mr Grimwig. The same man turned over my room, thinking I had something. You need to tell the police, Katie, about what happened and what he said.'

'They'll come soon enough when they find out I was her daughter-in-law. Do they know it was Davey that stole from the Grimwigs?'

'Not yet. But one of their top detectives is on the job. Katie, I need to find Davey before they do,' Mary pleaded. 'I know you know something…'

Katie sniffed and gazed into the distance, lost in her thoughts.

'If he had a scheme… and if he's running scared… he'd go to his mates in Wapping,' she said. 'But that's all I know, honest.'

'Did he ever talk about a fellow called Jankes?' Mary asked. 'A toff with a limp?'

Katie shook her head. 'Who's this Jankes?'

'Someone else who's after him,' Mary said.

'That doesn't surprise me. If he's cheated that Milverton, it's because someone else put him up to it. All I can say is try Wapping. That's where he'd hide. But where exactly…' she shook her head.

Mary reached inside her purse and began to take out some coins, only for Katie to place her hand on hers.

'Not a penny,' she said and lifted her head proudly, her mouth a firm straight line. 'We'll manage. Thanks for your kindness; it's not often I can say that,' and she closed the door.

Mary pitied her. Katie was alone with only her baby son for company. Even if Davey came back, she would still be alone. And if he didn't, her future lay elsewhere, in the awful expectations of the parish workhouse. What other recourse was left to her? Mary seethed with anger at the unfairness of it all as they walked away.

'Don't feel sorry for her,' Archie said. 'She's made her bed.'

'We should all feel sorry for her,' Mary said, sharply. 'This life is all she's ever known. I'm sure it wasn't the one she expected. I could have been her, Archie, if it wasn't for meeting Grandpa and Grandma. Who knows, I might have been dead by now, or far worse. It's not that she's made her bed as it is the only bed she's ever had.'

Archie looked down at the ground and mumbled he was sorry.

'I know you are, Archie. And I'm sorry as well and I hope something good will happen to her and Timmy – she needs a bit of luck.'

'She should have taken your money. God knows, she could use it.'

Pride is all she has left, Mary wanted to say, but she bit her tongue and kept quiet. When they reached the corner of the road, Archie nudged her. She followed his gaze.

Behind them, a hansom cab had turned into the street, stopping outside Katie Tupper's house. Inspector Lestrade and Constable O'Connor stepped out. Lestrade surveyed the tenement with a disdainful sneer and glanced around him at the sullen children. They watched him with distrustful faces from a safe distance. When O'Connor began walking towards them, they took to their heels. Lestrade watched them run, then knocked on the door and waited.

Mary knew he would tell Katie about her mother-in-law's death. He would ask where her husband was and would not be surprised to hear that she did not know. The bruises on her face, he would attribute to Davey because he'd probably seen such marks on many such women often enough.

But, Mary wondered, *when Katie tells him her husband's name, will the inspector remember our recent conversation?*

They walked quickly away towards Wapping, and as they did so, Mary glanced nervously from side to side. Her mind was busy with an awful truth: this was a dangerous game that had been forced on her. Since it had all started, when she had bumped into the thief, Mary had felt the danger was hers alone. Now she knew differently.

'How did the Bogeyman know about Mrs Tupper?' she asked. 'We knew about her from Emma. Milverton probably knew her from his dealings with Davey. So, how did Mr Grimwig know about her? It was his man that did for her – the man with the scar.' A heavy realisation settled in her stomach and made her queasy. 'I have a nasty feeling we led him to Mrs Tupper, Archie. Just like Mr Boots followed me that night, he, or more likely his friend with the scar, followed us to Whitechapel.'

'You're guessing,' Archie said. 'Anyway, you were in disguise, remember?'

Mary shook her head. 'It wasn't good enough, was it? Not if they found Mrs Tupper. And if Emma told them, then it was because they recognised me when we met. And I don't want to think about that, Archie. And since he's visited Katie, its because he knows Davey is the other man – my *accomplice*.'

'Is this why you're not wearing my old clothes?' Archie asked. Mary nodded sheepishly.

'It's what I figured this morning when you were reading that story.'

'You're still imagining ghosts,' Archie said. 'Scarface would stick out like a sore thumb. We'd have noticed if he was following us.'

'We never saw him when we visited Mrs Tupper.'

'*If* he was following us.'

'*He was.*'

They quickened their pace once they came to the main road, walking on in silence. Mary looked around but could see no one following. As Archie had said, the scarred man would be easily recognised. Her only consolation was that they were still one step ahead of the rest. Mr Grimwig, though, was determined to retrieve his property – Mrs Tupper's murder was proof of his resolve.

She was beginning to understand Mr Grimwig, although she lacked the resources to investigate him further. At least she could speculate; that much she had learned from Sherlock Holmes – she knew his methods.

How had someone from near poverty in a Manchester slum arrived at such giddy heights in so short a time? Mary remembered Mr Grimwig's fondness for relating his near-miraculous rise to fortune, often overhearing him speaking to his many guests.

'You'll never get rich by working for others,' he'd say. He had according to Inspector Lestrade, pulled himself up by his bootstraps. Grimwig epitomised success.

But he was a strange man and a dangerous one. His involvement with various charities was well known. He had ambitions in politics. He was fair in that his servants were never treated badly in his employment. He seemed content in his family life, supportive of his wife and indulgent with his children. However, there was another side to him that contradicted those lofty ideals. He could add murder to his list of achievements, because the man she'd seen with Mr Boots had killed Mrs Tupper.

20

DOT AND SOSSIE FIND THEM

They had gone no further than the top of the road when Mary turned around sharply. Archie stopped and glanced back with her.

'What the hell?' he said and threw his arms up in amazement.

Coming from around the corner of Katie's street, Dot and Sossie were haring towards them, a frightened panicked look darkening their faces. As they ran, they were constantly looking over their shoulders.

'It's the Bogeyman,' Sossie was shouting. 'Archie, Mary, it's him…' she was pointing to somewhere behind her.

They arrived, puffing and panting and Sossie kept on shouting. Their faces were red and glowing, their voices shrill with alarm.

‘What the hell are you two doing here?’ Archie bellowed.

‘Archie, it’s the Bogeyman,’ Sossie cried and the two sisters crowded as close to their brother as they could, repeating themselves several times and pointing behind to Katie’s street.

‘What are you going on about, Sossie?’ Archie asked angrily. ‘We took you two to school not a couple of hours ago, and you turn up here. Just what are you playing at?’

‘Archie, Archie, it’s–’

‘Yes, I heard.’

‘He’s been following you,’ Dot said nervously while glancing behind her.

‘That’s what we wanted to tell you,’ her sister said and tugged his sleeve hard.

‘What do you mean?’ Mary said and squatted down beside the frightened girls. She looked from where they had run, but could see no one. ‘Get your breath back and tell us.’

Both Dot and Sossie were trembling, and Mary placed her arms around their shoulders. They crowded nearer to her and held her arms tightly.

‘We saw him, the man with the scar and red eye, the one who burgled your room, when you left us at the school gate,’ Sossie said in a small and agitated voice.

‘He was following you,’ Dot said.

'We thought we could catch up and warn you–'

'–but you was walking too fast and he was too near and we couldn't get past him without him seeing us–'

'We didn't see you go in the library until you came out–'

'–then, that nasty policeman saw him and he ran away–'

'Let me get this right.' Archie looked around him, suddenly nervous, but he could not see anyone who fitted the girl's description. 'You two have been following us since we left you at the school? All the way here? And following a burglar as well?' He rolled his eyes in annoyance. 'Are you mad?'

'But Archie–' they said together.

'Don't you "but Archie" me. Didn't you know it was dangerous?'

'But Archie–' they said again pleadingly.

'I don't believe this,' Archie said. 'I ought to–'

'Archie!' Mary said quickly. 'They've been very brave. Naughty, yes, but brave nonetheless. I was worried we'd be followed today, and this confirms it. But he's away now and these two need to go back. It's best if you take them home and I'll go on to Wapping on my own.'

'No chance of that. I'm coming with you. As for these two...' Archie glowered at the frightened girls, '... you are going back home, you hear me?'

‘But we don’t know the way,’ Dot said and looked up in distress.

Archie huffed angrily.

‘Come here,’ he said and marched them to a nearby omnibus stop. He scanned the board with the destinations and looked down the street.

‘We’re sorry, Archie,’ they said quietly seeing how annoyed their brother was.

‘Come on, Archie,’ Mary said. ‘What they did shows how much they care,’ and she smiled at him.

Archie took in a deep breath and slowly shook his head. He knelt beside the girls, placed his arm around the two, drawing their sullen, anxious faces nearer to his, and hugged them.

‘Honestly, I swear I ain’t never seen anyone as annoying or daft as you two before. And if you weren’t my sisters, I’d have walloped your backsides by now. Don’t you know how dangerous what you did is? Mary and me can look after ourselves. You two can’t – that’s why you go to school – to get some brains. Look, the omnibus is coming. That one goes down Oxford Street. I’ll tell the man to make sure you two get off at Baker Street. Go home and stay home. God knows what you’re gonna tell Grandma when you should be in school – but don’t tell her about following no burglar, is that clear?’ They both nodded even though he was looking at Sossie.

'Nor about being up in Bow. She'd have a blue fit if she knew all that.'

'Here's a shilling each,' Mary said, 'in case of an emergency.'

'Archie, Archie,' Dot said excitedly, seeing the omnibus had an upstairs, 'can we sit on top?'

'Please, Archie,' Sossie pleaded.

He glared at them. Mary was about to say something and he glared at her as well, so she fell silent with a smirk on her face. Archie had a word with the conductor, paid their fares, and the two sullen-faced sisters climbed on board and sat in a mope on a bench seat inside. An elderly lady said she was going to Marble Arch and she would look after them and make sure they got off at Baker Street. With both she and the conductor looking after the girls, Archie felt happy they would be safe.

The conductor rang the bell. As they left, Mary could hear Sossie's shrill voice telling the elderly lady about the Bogeyman.

Mary turned to Archie and the boy grumped with a tight mouth.

'All right, all right, I was wrong,' he said. 'Scarface was following. But he ain't now that Inspector Lestrade's seen him off. Now, we walking to Wapping or catching a lift?'

'Walking,' Mary replied. 'I need to think.'

Being followed disturbed her, especially since she

had not seen anyone. The thought Scarface might still be following gave her goosebumps. Turning back wasn't an option, though; she couldn't do that now. She had a feeling that things were coming to a head and all her answers lay in the East End of London, a place she did not want to go, but had to.

21

WAPPING

Docks and warehouses dominated the waterfront of Wapping. Rank smells from the river permeated the air. The sounds of horns and hooters coming from the direction of the water told how busy it was, with brigs, scows, lighters, tugs, two and three-mast schooners and steamboats, and a multitude of other crafts plying their trade. Mary watched them with fascination, knowing that they brought African ivory, spices from India, rum and sugar from the Caribbean, Burmese hardwood, Norwegian softwood, silks and cotton, grain, tobacco and meat, and so much more besides. The list was endless – all to swell the coffers of government and business. The Port of London, she had read, had the busiest wharves in the world, and here international trade arrived twenty-four hours a day, seven days a week, fifty-two weeks a year, year in and year out; a relentless flow to the home of the Empire.

Mary knew that over the years Wapping had changed to keep pace with the march of commerce. Slums had been cleared and there were newspaper reports of plans to gain yet more space to build even more docks and warehouses. Even so, she saw how the streets narrowed and the dwellings became dark and rundown. Ship's chandlers, boat builders and sail lofts, mast, oar and block makers dotted about and mixed with workers cottages and tenements to inhabit the interior.

Her mind revelled and her heart fluttered in wonder. This was where she had to search, amongst streets busy with the comings and goings and the business of the river. She listened, fascinated, to the many different tongues of the folks whose fortune was to pitch up here, in the greatest docks of the world.

Brushing the snow off a broken-down wall, she sat down to rest her weary feet and marvelled at this fuss of humanity. It was noon and she and Archie had walked the three or so miles from Victoria Park. Add to that the distance from Baker Street and she was fatigued and hungry. She still had not got the new shoes she'd promised herself, and the soles of her feet ached.

Archie vanished, only to reappear a few minutes later with two portions of fish and chips wrapped in newspaper. Sitting on the wall, they ate in silence while sharing a bottle of ginger beer.

'That was good,' Mary said when they had finished. 'But a cup of tea would go down nice about now.'

'Can't help you there. Well, where do we start?' Archie asked and looked up and down the street.

'The pubs would be best. Better if we pretend we're related, brother and sister like, and act as if we're looking for our father–'

'–that'd be Davey Tupper I'm guessing–'

'–We just have to hope someone knows him and where he's at.'

Archie nodded to a public-house at the corner. 'The Old Dog's the nearest. I'll ask and you look pathetic and see what happens. Here, I never said: does Davey know you? Has he ever seen you?'

'Only when we bumped. Emma was particular about hiding him when he called. I know why now.' She glowered. 'It was less Emma hiding him, and more him that didn't want to be seen.'

Somewhere nearby was Davey Tupper. Where exactly, Mary did not know because Katie had not known. She remembered him from her brief encounter outside the Grimwigs' house – a man in his mid to late thirties, dark-haired, tanned and small with a weather-lined face. She recalled him as nervous and saw again the flash of anger in his eyes.

'Is this what your Mr Holmes would have done?' Archie joked.

'He'd only have got to the bottom of all this by now,' Mary moaned. 'He'd have got his man into Newgate jail already. But this isn't about thinking like Mr Holmes, this is about doing. And this'll be a long day, for sure.'

Sherlock Holmes was a thinker, that she knew, but even he, at times, had to resort to legwork when the need demanded, whether he did it himself or had others do it for him.

The Old Dog was a long, narrow building on the corner of the street. It leant its lopsided weight against the house next to it like a cripple leaning on a crutch. However, it gave the impression that it would not easily be removed. The paint was peeling, the wood was cracked, the windows were dark and grimy, yet it stood resolute. It looked old and set in its ways. Inside was dark and shadowy and lit by several oil lamps.

It took Mary some seconds for her vision to adjust to the gloom. Two groups of several boisterous dockworkers clustered around tables and drank away their wages. In a corner, two dusky men were deep in a singsong conversation with a couple of Orientals. A sharp-nosed woman was leaning on her elbows, whispering to a scruffy man by the window; by the door was a sullen-faced young man who looked decidedly troubled. The furniture was worn.

The air was fuggy with smoke from cigarettes and pipes and reeked of beer. It was stuffy and over warm.

Archie came up to what passed as the bar: several long planks of raw wood laid across trestles, behind which stood a short, fat, greasy hair man in a dirty shirt and trousers.

'What'll it be?' the man asked sharply.

'Excuse me, mister,' Archie said. 'We're looking for a man called Mr Tupper. Do you know him?'

The man leant on to the bar, supporting himself with his arms, the planks bending under his weight.

'Tupper, you say. What do you want with him?'

'We need to find him.'

'Why's that, then?' The barman eyed Archie suspiciously.

'Our mum's ill,' Mary said. 'She wants to see him before she passes.'

The barman fixed his eyes on her and Mary took on a sullen and pitiful expression. He looked her up and down, and then switched his view back to Archie and did the same. When he was satisfied with what he saw, he shouted out across the room to the sharp-nosed middle-aged woman by the window.

'Jenny, you seen Davey about?'

'The bruiser's popular today,' she shouted back and squinted in his direction. 'That makes two, don't it,

Sandy? The cripple and now those. Who wants to know this time.'

Mary mouthed '*Two?*' Archie shrugged.

'A couple of his brats, I shouldn't wonder,' the barman said dismissively.

Jenny stood up. She swayed as she walked, clearly drunk, and gripped the edge of a table to steady herself. She squinted again as if she needed spectacles. 'I ain't seen these ones before.'

'What? You seen 'em all, have you? Their mum's dying and they wants to find him.'

'Lost your dad, have you, son? That's blooming careless of you,' she laughed.

Archie smiled weakly. 'Me and my sister need to find him for our mum's sake.'

'Her and the others, I should imagine.'

'Do you know him?' Archie asked timidly.

'Oh! I know your dad, all right,' she sneered.

'Leave it out, Jenny and have some decency,' the barman said.

'Hark at who's speaking about decency,' she replied curtly. 'So, you're some of Davey's kids, are you? Who's your mum? Which one is she?'

'Foster,' Archie lied. 'Mrs Foster.'

'Ain't known that one.'

'From Deptford,' Mary added.

Jenny nodded. 'South, eh? How old are you, Mr

Foster, or is it Tupper? Sixteen, seventeen?' She eyed Archie. 'Well, you must be one of his first, I suppose. And his lot comes in all shapes and sizes, for sure, so you ain't no surprise. Don't suppose you'd care to buy me a drink, would you, Mr Foster?'

'Only if you know where we can find him.'

She laughed. 'Oh! You're one of Davey's, all right. Sorry, sonny, but your dad can rot in hell, as far as I'm concerned.' She opened her purse and turned it upside down and gave it a shake – nothing fell out of it. 'I figured if you're one of his you owe me a drink at least since he's taken everything I own – one of his get rich schemes!' she huffed contemptuously. 'No sonny, I've no idea where the goat is if he ain't dead–'

'Jenny!' the barman said crossly.

She scowled and went back to the man she had been talking to. 'He's one for the hangman…' she mumbled.

'Ignore her,' the barman said. 'I forgot she and him don't get on anymore. Your dad's around somewhere, son, I saw him a month ago. Try the pubs down by the water.'

'Thanks, mister,' Mary said. 'Did you say someone else's looking for him?'

'I didn't say that, missy,' the barman said. 'But it seems as if Davey's coming up in the world if he's keeping company with silk and satin.'

‘Was it an elderly gent with glasses and a silver-tipped cane?’ she asked.

‘No, not old. He carried a cane, all right; he needed one with his gammy leg. Here, try Payton Norris over there; he runs for him. Payton, didn’t you take that friend of Davey’s to see him? The crippled one this morning?’

The sullen-faced youth by the door, his iron-grey hair thinning and eyes wide, glanced up furtively. Mary had noticed him watching them when Jenny came over. He had turned his head slightly away, but she knew he had been listening. He said nothing, but became instantly nervous when the barman called him.

‘Payton, I asked if you–’

The youth jerked and quickly arose as if stung by a wasp. His face had coloured up a vivid red. He muttered various curses. In an awkward nervous rush, he hurriedly left the pub.

‘Payton! Payton!’ the barman shouted, but the young man had gone. ‘Some folks are queer,’ he said to Archie, ‘leaving good beer behind.’

Mary and Archie quickly left to follow, but Payton had turned down an alley, and when they reached it, they saw it led to several others. He was gone.

‘At least we’re in the right place,’ Mary said as they started towards the buildings nearer the water.

‘Someone else’s looking for him,’ Archie reminded Mary.

‘It sounded like Jankes – a toff with a limp.’

‘How did he know where to look?’ Archie asked.

‘I don’t know. But when he asked me if I knew Davey, I got the impression that *he* knew him as well.’ Mary chewed her lip. ‘What did Lestrade call Jankes? An opportunist?’

In the next few hours, they visited one pub after the other. They walked east towards Limehouse, rounding the Surrey bend in the river, heading towards the docks and wharves at Millwall. By early evening, they had arrived at Blackwall Reach, finally stopping at Bow Creek. It had been a fruitless search with regards to finding Davey Tupper. However, more details about the thief had emerged as if from a mist.

Someone had described him as a pickpocket with ambition. By all accounts, all of his dealings were illegal. Like the landlord of The Crown, people knew him, but were cautious about saying too much. There was something dark about him that made people speak with a warning in their voices. The police sought him, but lacked the evidence for an arrest. He had eluded them more through luck than design. Mary wondered how Emma, let alone Katie and Jenny in The Old Dog, could have fallen for such a man. And as Archie said, Davey Tupper seemed quick with his fists.

They found a spot on the quayside cleared of snow and sat dangling their legs over the edge of the riverbank.

In the eddying evening tide and the sinking sun, the murky waters of the Thames looked brown and oily with a film of dust on the surface. Mary leaned back on her elbows. It had been only a few days since the start of this business. She took stock. Was she any nearer? The pieces were fitting together. She had understood the chain of events that had led her here, to the riverside docks. Then she remembered Jankes and the Earl of Marshmere. Things were making sense.

Archie asked her what they would do if and when they found Davey, and she still did not have a clear answer. She would have to play it by ear when that time came, that much she knew. But then, her choices were limited. She considered. If she found the thief, could she then go to the police? They had not believed her then, that first night; would they do so now? Lestrade had made his thoughts clear enough. She had only herself to fall back on – and Archie as well.

22

MARY, THE BOY AND THE THIEF

Mary stirred as the chimes from a nearby church announced seven o'clock. The sky was black. Across the river, the lights of Rotherhithe and Greenwich burned brightly. The traffic on the water had navigation lanterns lit. Red, green and white lights, hanging from invisible masts and spars, danced over and along the Thames, their shimmering reflected in the murky river, while below them, vague silhouettes cut through the dark water leaving pale, silent wakes. The river slapped against the banks in a disorderly rhythm, while from all around came the muffled sounds from the alehouses of Blackwall. The air, fed by the thin, damp mist that drifted across the water, became icy. Mary and Archie pulled their coats tighter against a breeze that brought with it a cold that could penetrate the soul.

It had been, as she'd predicted, a long day, and she was about ready to set off for home with its promise of warmth and food when the boy approached them. He might have been ten, dressed in patched clothes and muddy shoes. He was a thin bandy-legged boy, with a sunken dirty face and straggly, greasy hair – she remembered Dr Watson using a very distinctive adjective to describe such children. He stood five feet away from them, saying nothing, just watching.

Mary had seen the boy several times during the day. She'd paid him little attention then, but now, as he stood beside them, she realised that he had been trailing them. Perhaps, she thought, he had been getting up the courage to speak and beg for a few coins, hence his furtive behaviour.

Instead, he stood quiet in his nervousness. Occasionally, he would glance behind or to the sides before resuming his vigil. He remained always just out of arm's reach, as if ready to run at the slightest provocation. Mary waited for him to make up his mind.

'You looking for Mr Tupper?' the boy said eventually.

'Know him?' Archie asked.

'Might do.'

'You do or you don't.' Archie's voice was sharp with tiredness.

The boy quietly chewed his lower lip.

'Might do,' he said after a while.

'Yes, we're looking for Mr Tupper,' Archie said in an offhand manner. 'You know where he is?'

'Might do.'

Archie shrugged at Mary and turned back to the boy.

'You don't say much, do you? All right, where is he?' he asked.

The boy held out a hand. Archie considered him with a steady eye, and then grinned. He took a sixpence from his pocket and held it out towards him. The boy hesitated. He reached forward slowly, and then quickly snatched the coin. Smiling, no doubt pleased with himself, the boy first looked closely at the sixpence, as if deciding if it was real or fake, and then, satisfied, placed it inside a pocket. As before, he stood like a quiet sentry once again.

'Well?' Archie said.

The boy remained silent.

Archie sighed and took out another sixpence and held it out towards the boy. Again, the boy's hand reached slowly towards the coin. He tried to snatch it, but Archie flicked his wrist out of the way and the boy's hand grasped nothing. With that, the boy withdrew his hand.

Archie proffered the coin again.

'Well?' Mary asked.

The boy's eyes fixed the coin.

'Do you want it or not?' she said.

'Might do.'

Archie sighed. 'Well, it's all there is. It ain't going to have any more babies.'

'What do you want him for?' the boy asked.

'That's our business. Make your mind up or give me back my sixpence.'

'He's our dad,' Mary said, weary at having to say it again.

The boy looked over his shoulders and into the darkness several times as if fearing some interruption. He held out his hand once more. Archie deposited the coin into his palm. The boy flicked his head to indicate a direction behind him, to say, '*Come on*!' and began walking. Mary and Archie followed as he wandered off, heading back towards Limehouse.

He led them in a more or less westerly direction across the Isle of Dogs. Every now and then, he would stop, wait, and then carry on again. Eventually, they emerged from a series of closely housed streets to the waterfront. In all that time, the boy had not spoken a word.

Once they reached the river, he began to fidget. He bounced from one foot to the other and again chewed his lower lip; he seemed to be nervously waiting.

'Are we here?' Mary asked, but the boy did not answer. 'Are we here?' she asked louder.

The boy's head jerked as if remembering who was

with him. He turned his face to her and smiled. It was an awkward, fawning smile and it made Mary instantly anxious.

'I don't like this, Archie,' she said.

'Me neither. Just wish we had some more light.'

Mary could see little. Behind her, the warehouses were shadows against a black sky. The silent, smoke-stained wooden buildings, large and dull, frowned at them. They rose from the quayside and seemed to lean over and across, closing out any stray light and lending their weight to the already heavy, murky air. The path in front of the buildings was empty of people and disappeared into the gloomy shadows of the river air on either side. Only the lapping water broke the heavy quiet around them.

'Is this where Tupper is?' Mary asked sternly. She was annoyed and wondered what was wrong with the boy. Was he simple? Had he just led them around, aimlessly, to keep the shilling Archie had given him?

The boy stepped away and back two paces. He raised his arm and pointed to a side door in one of the buildings.

'In there?' Archie asked. It looked a dark, unwelcoming place. The boy nodded. 'Is he there now?' and the boy shrugged. Archie growled at him.

Mary approached the door slowly and carefully. She hesitated and glanced back. The boy, clearly agitated, squirmed restlessly. The feeling that something was not right intensified. She grasped the handle on the door, twisted it only to realise that it was locked. Again, she looked back at the boy as if to ask if this was where he meant.

The clouds cleared, and in the moon's half-light, Mary could see the boy biting his lip furiously. She turned back to the door. Nails secured it against the frame, holding it firm. It could not be opened.

The hairs on the nape of her neck prickled. Surely the boy knew that? The realisation that he did made her heart jump. She startled and quickly turned to question him.

The boy backed away in hesitant steps. He had tensed. His head flicked from side to side. Soon, his gaze stopped on Mary's face. His eyes betrayed his fear, and suddenly he was running, his footsteps clattering and echoing as he dashed across the cobbles, his arms and legs flailing wildly.

'There goes a shilling,' Archie moaned. 'Well, let's see what's there,' and he started to walk to the door.

'Something's wrong,' Mary shouted. She grabbed his arm. 'It's a trap. Archie, we need to go. Now!'

Suddenly, the clatter of the boy's running stopped. Mary's head shot up. A man came out from the shadow of a building to meet him. The boy pointed. The man looked, and then sprinted towards them.

In an instant, Mary and Archie turned and began running away from him. They had gone no more than a few steps when two other men appeared in front of them, stepping apart to block any escape, trapping them.

There was the mouth of an alley between the warehouses. Archie grasped Mary's wrist and pulled her towards it. The moment they entered the alley, they could see it was blocked. Raw lumber was piled high, filling the sides of the path to the walls of the buildings. It was impossible to go around it, and to go over it in the half-light was far too dangerous.

They glanced around, seeking a door or a means to enter the warehouses and escape. There was none.

Behind them, the sounds of running feet had turned into the slow clip-clopping of heels against the stone as the men ambled towards them. There was no escape through the alley, so they were taking their time.

Mary pulled Archie along, attempting to run back towards the river. But as they broke out on to the quayside, the men were standing in front of them in a semi-circle. Mary and Archie retreated several steps.

'You took your time, I must say,' one of the men said looking at Mary.

The smallest of the three men carried an oil lantern. He turned up the wick and raised it high. When Mary saw it was Payton Norris, the youth from The Old Dog, she took a step back. A frightened nervousness inhabited his face. At the same time, she noticed the knife held by the one who had spoken.

'I'd almost given up hope,' he said, his voice laughing as a smile appeared on his shadowy face. 'I thought maybe young Georgie had lost the way. I thought maybe we'd have to go and find you.'

23

DAVEY TUPPER

Mary and Archie cowered a step back.

'Who are you?' Mary asked. 'What do you want?'

'Those are my questions,' the man with the knife said. 'You two have been dogging me since this morning. I'd like to know why. Neither of you is any brood of mine, at least that I know of. As to your ailing mother,' he sneered, 'I ain't never heard of any Foster – Mister or Missus.'

When Payton raised the lantern higher, Mary saw she was looking into the dark eyes of the thief she'd run into outside the Grimwigs' house – Davey Tupper. She remembered the face well. She remembered how he'd glared at her that night. Then, the stranger had looked nervous and skittish. But now his face was as hard as flint and the fear had been replaced by menace. His gaze was cold. His black deep-set eyes were icy as the river air.

To his left stood Payton Norris, his face shining with sweat. His tense, nervous gaze fell all around and about; he seemed unable to keep still for a second. On Tupper's right stood another nervous man with the same unmistakable features as Payton. He had to be an older brother, though he was a good deal taller. They both glanced apprehensively towards Davey Tupper.

'You did well, Georgie.' Tupper's lips twisted and curled. On hearing his name, the boy ran up to Tupper. He stood behind the men, watching in his silent way, the odd wide grin spread across his face, thoroughly pleased with himself.

The thief reached inside his pocket and took out a shilling and flicked it to the boy. The boy's hands shot up, snapping at it like a trout at a fly, but he missed and the coin rattled onto the cobblestones. He immediately dropped on to his knees, his arms darting out and his fingers clutching it as it bounced.

'Be off with you,' the thief said.

The boy stood up with his catch. Remaining where he was, he lifted the coin to his eyes and smirked at Mary, and then carefully put it inside his pocket, where he had placed Archie's money.

'Get off with you,' Tupper bellowed.

As if stung, the boy jerked, turned and ran, his feet

clattering across the cobbles and he was away. When he turned the corner, the thief gave a low curse. Some men were approaching along the quayside. Their voices were raised and their feet clacked heavily against the cobblestone as they came nearer.

Tupper quickly advanced towards Mary. She stood her ground, knowing that she could not retreat, wanting to scream for help. But her mouth was dry. Before she could even try, the thief's hand came up and grasped her throat. Even so, she tried to shout, but he pinched harder, snuffing her cry. Her hands came up and prised at his fingers. As if answering her efforts, the sharp point of a blade jabbed against her ribs. She flinched and stopped fighting, dreading what the thief might do if she made a sound.

Tupper dragged her into the alley and leant his weight on her, pinning her up against the wall. Before Archie could intervene, he too was jostled and shoved and pushed back into the gap between the buildings. Payton Norris blew out the wick of the lamp, and the world inside the alley went black.

'Don't think about it, boy,' Tupper whispered hoarsely to Archie. 'Make a sound and you know what'll happen.' He held the knife up so Archie could see the glint of the blade.

'I'll not have anything more to do with murder,' Payton hissed.

'Shut it!' Tupper scowled. 'It's a little late for that, ain't it?'

'Damn you,' the other man said. 'Do you hear me, Tupper?'

'You can shut it as well, Tom,' came the angry reply.

The men were coming nearer. Their voices were getting louder. They were laughing, telling jokes and making fun, probably going home from the pub. Tupper held Mary tightly. He dropped his head until it was a few inches above hers, his foul breath blowing into her face. His grip tightened and she choked back a wave of nausea, struggling to stand upright. Beads of sweat trickle down her back. She gasped for breath.

'Not one sound, girl,' he whispered.

The drunken party reached them. Still joking and roaring and singing, they swept past. In despair, Mary could hear their footsteps moving away. Her fearful eyes followed them as they clacked along the quayside. The further they went, the more her hopes diminished. Soon their laughter faded into the heavy gloom, getting fainter and more distant, disappearing. And then they were gone.

She gazed in trepidation back to the thief and saw him glance in both directions along the quayside.

'Take them up to the room,' Tupper said.

'Davey, I said…' A vicious look from the thief silenced the man called Tom. For a second, the two of them stared bitterly at each other.

Tupper held Mary tightly as they walked towards a run-down building by the water's edge. It had once possibly been a warehouse; its upper storeys overhung the river in a series of steps, but it had seen better days and quietly awaited its fate. Neglect and damp had rotted the piles on which it stood and left it leaning precariously out towards the water, almost bending over and about to totter into the Thames. It looked unsavoury, cold and desolate, decidedly unsafe, a refuge for the desperate, and somewhere Mary did not want to be. But she had little choice now as she stood in front of it.

Payton Norris opened the door, as excitable as a nervous schoolboy. He glanced to his brother for courage. Once the oil lamp was lit, they went inside. They climbed the stairs that came out into a passageway, the stairs continuing upwards from the landing into deep shadows. Before reaching the next floor, the flight became shattered and broken and impassable.

It was only then that Tupper released his hold on Mary. There was nowhere to run. He pushed her forward, the only direction she could go.

The dark, musty, creaky passageway led to a room at its end. The oil lamp was sufficient to show that the room was bare but for three old, stained mattresses with blankets in a corner, and a table and two chairs in the middle. Three separate piles of clothes lay beside the beds. Several bottles of liquor rested on the table.

Empty bottles, old newspapers, bits of broken furniture lay strewn across the floor. The air was rank with the smell of rotten food and rat droppings, and the stink of the river was a fetid miasma. It was a dismal place. But it was here that the three men slept, or so Mary assumed.

On the far wall, a boarded-up window gazed blindly across the Thames. Just below the window, the wooden floor had fallen away. A wide section gaped black, and through it, the waters of the river could be heard lap-lapping against the piles and reflected, glittering, fish-scale shimmering, on to the ceiling. Beside the hole and in the shadows, a dark shape leant crookedly against the wall, as if a sack had been carelessly thrown there.

The next moment, Archie cursed. He looked mortified. His eyes shot across to Mary. When she saw why, she recoiled in horror and quickly looked away. A tingle ran up her spine.

Slumped on his side, half-covered by a blanket, was a man. He stared back at them through glazed eyes. His legs were drawn up to his chest, his arms wrapped around them. He looked peaceful, dressed in clothes of fine silk and cotton, and had his eyes been closed, his empty face could well have been mistaken for sleeping. But they gazed back, unblinking orbs, peering unseeing into the room. The paleness of his skin, even under the warm glow of the oil lamp, the trickle of blood soaking the floor with a dark stain in which he lay, and his unmoving stiffness told the tale.

He was dead.

A cruel pleasure caused the thief to grin.

'Meet Mr Jankes,' he said and winked.

24
A REGULAR SHERLOCK HOLMES

Mary struggled to drag her eyes away from the man she'd only recently met. Her heart leapt in her chest. Tupper pushed her to the centre of the room and closed the door behind him.

'Is he dead?' Mary asked. Her voice trembled – she already knew the answer.

'I know you,' Tupper said. He took the lamp from Payton and brought it nearer. Mary lifted her face so that it caught the light and removed the shawl from around her head. His eyes narrowed to a squint. An odd smile curled his lips and he nodded as if remembering.

'It was me you bumped into when you stole from the Grimwigs that night,' Mary said. 'It was me that picked up the jewels you dropped. It was me that got the push because they thought we were in the robbery together.'

Tom scowled. 'You were an idiot, taking those damned jewels.'

'They were there to be lifted.' Davey Tupper's eyes flicked darkly.

'You should have stuck to Jankes's plan,' Tom said. 'He would be doing the business now if you did. Jankes said–'

'Jankes said, Jankes said… well he ain't saying nothing now, is he?' Tupper reached over to pick up the dead man's walking stick. 'Now you listen to me,' he scowled angrily, 'it was me that did the work. I was the one that nearly got caught.' He brought the stick down on the table. It banged like a gunshot and Mary jumped as the report echoed inside the room. 'Now don't you be telling me what I should and shouldn't be doing, like you're *Mr Jankes*.'

Tupper held the cane high as a warning. It obviously troubled Payton as the man could not look directly at the thief. Clearly, the brothers did not trust him.

The thief turned back to Mary. 'So, what is it you want?'

Mary swallowed her fears. Her voice was firm, even if she trembled inside.

'My name cleared for a start,' she announced boldly. 'Failing that, some of what you took from the Grimwigs.'

Archie's mouth dropped open, and both the thief and Tom eyed her in surprise.

'Well, aren't you the game one?' Tupper said. 'And what did I take that you want some of? Not them gems, that's for sure.'

'No, you messed that up, didn't you?' Mary said acidly. 'And you almost got me arrested.'

Her boldness seemed to take the thief by surprise. She saw the puzzled look on his face. Mary calmly brushed her dress straight and took time to adjust the pleats back in line, keeping him waiting. She had to be fearless – nothing else would do.

'Milverton sent us to find you.' Her heart leapt when she saw how Davey Tupper's head jerked at the mention of the name. It was fear she saw in his eyes. Now she knew she had been right to be bold. 'He's got a message for you. He *expects* his deal to be honoured. He's paid good money, and in advance, and he demands a return on his investment. I don't think he's a charitable man – do you?'

'How comes he never told me about you?' Tupper asked cautiously.

'Tell the help?' Mary was scornful. 'He never did trust you. He had me keep an eye on things. Except I was out that day when you came. But I never thought you'd be stupid enough to try it when the Grimwigs were in. Or dumb enough to take his wife's gems as well.'

Davey Tupper gripped the cane tighter. He was not used to being talked to like that. Mary felt the bile rise in her throat and wondered if she had gone too far. She kept her gaze fixed on him, because to look away now would be a mistake.

'If he didn't trust me, why didn't he get you to thieve the letters?' he said.

Mary smiled ruefully – she had guessed correctly.

'He should have. I wouldn't have messed it up.' She lifted her head higher still. 'He has other plans for me, see. There are other households he wants me to work, and for that, he needs to keep my name clean. That's why you and me never met when you visited Emma. But you ruined that for him, and me, didn't you? And he ain't at all pleased after all the work he's put in.' Slowly and menacingly, she said, 'He wants the letters – he's paid for them, and he means to get them one way or another.'

The thief's eyes flicked away from hers and Mary smiled inwardly. The more doubt she could sow, the greater their chances of leaving this place alive.

'Is she telling the truth, Davey?' Tom Norris's voice betrayed his dread.

'I know it all,' Mary said firmly. 'I know you don't go from a slum in Manchester to a house in Regent's Park so quickly by polite means; you do it by blackmailing an Earl. Marshmere's affair with Mrs G wouldn't go down so well in high society, if it were ever known. Milverton and me know the Earl fears his wife – she's the one with the power and the connections. That's why Marshmere pays well for Grimwig's silence. It's her money that made him, it's her money that'll break him.'

No one was interrupting her. She felt emboldened.

'God knows what she'll do if she finds out how much he's already handed over to the Grimwigs. If she does, he knows she'll cut him loose without a penny and feed him to the dogs.' Mary folded her arms haughtily and carried on quietly, as if musing to herself. 'Who knows, maybe the triplets are the Earl's? Fits, don't it? They're eleven. Eleven years ago was when the Grimwigs started their social climbing, wasn't it?'

'The brats are his?' Tupper said. Mary had no reason to think otherwise. It was something else to throw on the table.

'As for the Grimwigs,' Mary continued, as brazenly as before, 'they're worried it'll all come out. They'll pay up for the letters, because the letters will make it easy to prove how he got his wealth. Then jail will be the least of their worries. And Milverton knows that none of you–' Mary nodded at Tupper and the brothers in turn '–is clever enough to cheat him. He knows about *him.*' She nodded bullishly to the body of Jankes, wondering if he had seized the opportunity to get rich and out from under the control of the Earl when he discovered this scheme. But Jankes hadn't reckoned on Davey Tupper's greed.

She caught Tom Norris's gaze and held it firmly in hers. He blinked nervously.

'Blackmail the Grimwigs and the Earl if you want, but to leave Milverton out of it is a mistake. At best, he could let the police deal with you. What's he got to lose? There's nothing here that can come back to him.' She turned her gaze on Payton who stood stiffly, his elbows drawn in tightly to his sides 'And you try ratting on Milverton, try telling the coppers and see where that gets you – a one-way ticket to the cemetery. Not that you can prove anything. He's clever that way.' She turned to the thief. 'Worst case is when he catches up with you – which he will, even if it takes a year and a day. It was him that told us where to look. Believe me, the Peelers or Milverton's men will find you easier than we did.'

Mary's knees were trembling, but she could see in Tupper's eyes that her bluff had made him think. His tongue flicked incessantly across his dry lips, a pulse twitching in his neck.

'A regular Sherlock Holmes, aren't you?' He took out a bundle of papers tied with a scarlet ribbon and threw them on to the table. 'Do you figure I owe you a cut, like Jankes over there?'

'You owe me nothing,' Mary scoffed. 'But I ain't brave enough to cross Milverton. Boasting to Katie and your mum?' she sneered. 'That wasn't clever, especially after what's happened to them.' Tupper looked puzzled, but Mary continued to speak, 'And here we are! Grimwig's man after you. Milverton also. Marshmere as well, when he finds out Jankes is dead. And let's not forget the coppers – that makes it a right little circus, don't it?'

'Grimwig's man? Katie? My mum? What you on about?' Tupper grabbed her wrist.

'She's dead,' Mary shouted as she winced in pain. 'Your mother. Murdered. It was in the morning's papers. Strangled in her house in Hanbury Street. Grimwig's man did for her and beat up Katie. He even threatened your son. The last thing your mum saw was the evil scar-faced man choking the life out of her, staring with his red eye.'

Tupper's voice broke in fright. 'Black Bob? He's Grimwig's man? A scar and one red eye?'

'That's him.' Mary twisted her hand free and stepped back, rubbing her wrist. 'Black Bob. He almost did for me as well.'

'He's a terrier, that one,' Tupper said, breathing hard and speaking as if to himself. 'Once he gets his teeth in, he don't let go. Grimwig's cutting up rough, damn him.'

'Davey, your mum's–'

'If she's dead, she's dead, ain't she?' Tupper shouted over Tom, but fear coloured his voice. 'Ain't nothing more I can do for her, is there? We've got more trouble than her.'

He turned back towards Mary and Archie.

'No way. Not again,' Tom said.

'Stop being stupid – we made a deal. In for a penny,

remember?' Tupper scowled. 'You didn't complain about Jankes, did you?'

'That was different,' Payton said. 'I'm not having any more to do with murder.'

'Me neither – not a girl.' Tom ran his fingers through his hair and wiped the sweat from his forehead with his sleeve. 'It wasn't us that did him.'

'No, you both stood and watched,' Tupper snapped. 'Both of you wants to ride in carriages, wants maids and butlers to fetch and carry, wants your slippers and smoking jackets and brandy by the fire. Wants what Grimwig's got. How do you think he got it? By being nice, or by crossing his "T"s and dotting his "I"s? A secret's best kept if only a few know it, and the fewer, the better.'

He took a step towards Mary and Archie.

'You'll swing for it,' Mary said.

'Then we'll swing for it – for Jankes or for you, does it matter which?'

'I ain't swinging for no one.' Tom grabbed the thief's arm and dragged him away. 'Listen to me, killing them doesn't solve our problem if Bob's on our trail. If Milverton told her where to look, then he won't be far behind, either.'

'I didn't think I'd shipped out with such yellow muck as you two.' The menace in Davey Tupper's voice made Tom flinch. Even so, the thief retreated a step. 'So, what do you propose? You like thinking. What do you *think* we should do?'

Tom looked to his brother for support, but Payton would not look at him. In the heavy silence, Mary could hear the pounding of her heart.

'If you kill us, then you'll never have a moment of peace,' she said quietly, swallowing hard to hide the desperation in her voice. 'Tom's right. Milverton will find and kill you just as an example to anyone else thinking they can double-cross him. Grimwig will do you just out of spite. Or the law will hang you.' She caught Tom's eyes. 'Your only hope is to make a deal with Milverton. Me and Archie is the go-betweens you need. He trusts me. It's your only chance if you want to get something out of this – and stay alive.'

Tom seemed lost and unsure, his breathing sharp and harsh. He swung his gaze back to Mary and Archie and pointed to the corner where the beds were.

'Get over there, you two. Sit down and shut up,' he said.

'The tide's running, ain't it?' Tupper said, and walked slowly across the room to the dead body. 'It's gone eight, ain't it? Let's deal with this problem first while we've got the tide.'

He looked at Payton and, with a nod of his head, beckoned the youth over. Payton shook his head and glanced down to the floor.

‘Precious, ain’t we?’ the thief said. ‘He won’t bite. He’s past that.’ He swore when the man refused to move. ‘You and me, Tom. Come on, let’s see if you’re made of sterner stuff.’ He snorted at Payton. ‘Stand by the door, *boy*, and make sure these two don’t run away. If you can manage that,’ he mocked.

Tom came reluctantly. His face looked yellow and his lips trembled. He knelt beside the body and reached out hesitantly. When he saw the sneer on Tupper’s face, his mouth tightened and he grasped Jankes’s arm firmly. Together, they heaved and dragged the dead man to the opening where the floor had fallen away.

‘Stiff as a board!’ Tupper cursed.

They edged Jankes through the hole. There was a dull splash, and then a heavy silence.

‘The tide’ll take him past the Reach by morning,’ Tupper said, wiping the sweat from his forehead. ‘With any luck, past Woolwich before they find him – if they find him and he don’t sink first.’

25

A FALLING OUT OF THIEVES

Tom Norris stared ahead of him at nothing in particular. His eyes crawled sideways, met Mary's hard, impassive glare and flicked away. Mary could see his fears. He seemed to have collapsed and become a limp rag.

'I didn't kill him,' he mumbled, as if speaking to himself.

The thief grasped a bottle of gin from the table. He thrust it towards Tom who turned away, unable to look at his dark face. Tupper jeered and leant against the opposite wall from the beds and slowly slid down until he was seated with his legs drawn up. He took a long draught. His eyes smouldered as they met Mary's.

She held her panic in check and gazed back defiantly. When Davey Tupper drank, she nudged Archie and motioned with her head to the hole in the floor. Archie looked over. If they had to, Mary's eyes said, they'd jump through it and take their chances there. Archie gave a slight nod.

Payton Norris slumped into a chair next to his brother and rested his elbows on the table. His fingers fidgeted and he shuffled uncomfortably. He bit his lips every time his eyes strayed to where Jankes's body had been.

When he looked up, he saw the thief was gazing at him. Payton choked back a nervous giggle that grew in his mouth and swallowed it whole.

Tupper sighed, took another drink, shook his head slowly and clucked his lips. For several minutes, he sat silently, supping at the bottle.

Mary both feared and revelled in the idea that he was getting drunk. If he drank enough, she did not doubt she could convince Tom and Payton Norris to let them go. She saw how afraid they were. But with enough drink, Tupper could become unpredictable, the outcome uncertain. The chance that she and Archie might die stole into her thoughts. She needed to focus her mind.

'There's too much at stake for hangers-on, Tom,' the thief said, his face stern. 'And we've gone too far already. What with Black Bob trailing us – you think I'm dangerous? You ain't seen him. A black-hearted rogue as ever lived. And I never trusted that Milverton. He's dangerous, too, but for different reasons. All smooth and suave as if butter wouldn't melt in his mouth–' Tupper's voice was scornful. 'We need to send him a message, let him know what'll happen if he tries it on with us.'

'I'm not having anything more to do with cold-blooded murder,' Payton mumbled.

'Cold, warm, hot,' Tupper said. 'Murder is murder as far as the law is concerned, boy, no matter what the temperature.'

'No one knows we did Jankes – you said he might never be found.'

'No one but us, and those two. And I don't like sharing with that many.' Tupper took another swig and jabbed his head towards the letters. 'I did the graft. I took the risk. I ain't letting anyone reap the reward.'

'The jewels were where you went wrong,' Mary said to Tupper, her voice cold and clinical. He glanced at her with the same angry look he'd had when they met in the snow outside Mr Grimwig's residence. 'Taking them was a mistake – them being missing was discovered too quickly. What the Grimwigs didn't want to happen – Milverton nor Jankes too, I'd guess – was the police to get involved. If you'd only took the letters, it would have been days, weeks even, before anyone knew they were gone. That would've given you plenty of time to set up the blackmail.'

'You're a clever one, ain't you?' Tupper said scornfully. 'Maybe I should have had you as a partner instead of these two.'

Mary huffed. 'I only works for the best.' The thief sneered. 'Now you're having to rush everything and it's all gone wrong. You need Milverton, and us.' Mary glanced to Tom Norris. 'What do any of you know about doing blackmail properly? That's Milverton's game; he's the expert. You can still come out of this rich if I make a deal for you with him.'

There was a glimmer in Tom's eyes that told her he believed her. Whatever he decided to do, his brother would agree. But Davey Tupper was a different proposition.

'I don't need you or Milverton,' Tupper said tersely.

Payton, unable to quieten his fingers, picked up the ribbon-tied parcel.

'I don't get it,' he said. 'What harm is in these letters to make us rich?'

'Or swing,' Mary said.

'Shut up, you hear me?' Payton barked and threw the parcel down as if the letters were poisonous and the venom had burned him. Mary gloated, hearing the dread in his voice. The thief, though, took yet another swig.

'You really need to learn to read, boy. Then you might become as clever as *her*. Maybe that's what you should do when we get our first payment – get someone to teach you. The gentleman writes charmingly, for sure. But then you'd expect that from an Earl.' He laughed. 'Yes, but he was stupid as well. He didn't know the

Grimwigs. They set him up royal proper. You never did wonder how they got that mill or that big house and servants in Regent's Park, did you, boy?'

Payton shook his head. Tupper hung his own and smiled smugly.

'Same way we're gonna get ours. Except we've got both the Earl and the Grimwigs as benefactors. Two for the price of one. That's the beauty of this scheme, boy. Isn't that so, Tom? And why do you want to spoil that?'

Tom's silence told Mary what she already knew. She saw how Jankes's presence haunted the room in the furtive glance the brothers exchanged. But his silence wasn't lost on the thief, either.

'Now, don't you go soft on me, Tom. This is the game, like it or not. And I'm for doing the business now rather than later,' and his eyes fell on Mary and Archie, the drink making them seem darker than ever. His speech was slurred.

In his narrowing gaze, Mary knew she was losing the battle. She glanced at the opening in the floor and wondered if she and Archie could get there quicker than Davey could reach them. It was no more than a few steps. She guessed that neither Tom nor Payton would try to stop them. One quick rush and she and Archie would be through. Her legs trembled as she drew them up in a crouch. But Tupper was watching her and Mary wondered if he had guessed her plan.

He proffered the bottle to Tom. 'Come on, boy, Dutch courage.' Tom gave him a disdainful look and the thief sneered. 'More for me then.'

He finished the bottle, drained the last drop and flung it away. It clattered noisily across the floor, and both Tom and Payton's eyes followed it as it fell through the gap and splashed into the waters below.

'The hangman's drop,' Mary said and saw their eyes flash across to each other.

The thief laughed quietly.

'The tide's running, Tom,' he said, nodding at the hole in the floor where the bottle had disappeared. 'It's either now, or we'll lose it and have to leave it till tomorrow night when it's dark – and that's too long for me. If you ain't up for the deed, I am.'

The words dropped slowly off his tongue and hung in the air. A bitter smile clung to his lips, a coldness came to his eyes. Davey Tupper rose in a stumble and leant against the wall for support. His icy stare fixed on Mary. His mouth pursed. His brow furrowed. He had made his mind up; as he stepped forward, he was holding the knife.

Time had run out.

26

BLACK BOB

'Are you lot idiots?' Mary screamed in desperation. She and Archie had retreated as far as they could. 'You think Tupper'll be satisfied with a third share? When he's through with us, who'll be next? You, Payton? You, Tom? He wants it all for himself. Can't you see that?'

'You shut your trap,' Tupper shouted.

'Remember what he said? He don't like sharing. The best way to keep a secret is to make sure no one knows about it. Well, there's lots here that knows it,' she cried, trying to keep the brothers on her side. 'Not just Archie and me. But you, Payton. And you, Tom.

'That's what you said,' Payton shouted at Tupper.

'And that's too many for his liking.'

'Tom – isn't that what he said?'

Tom and Payton Norris slowly stepped back one

pace. The thief's knife was hypnotic as it swayed before their eyes. They were afraid.

Tupper shouted, 'Don't listen to her, you fools. When have I done you wrong? Can't you see what she's trying to do?'

'He crossed Milverton and Jankes, didn't he?' Mary was relentless. 'He killed Jankes, didn't he? Who else will he kill after us?'

She left the question hanging and, in the heavy silence, watched the brothers eye each other as a shadow passed across their faces. They had probably never trusted Davey Tupper. Then Mary carried on speaking, knowing that her and Archie's lives hung on a thread.

'And you think the Grimwigs will let it rest? Do they already know you're involved, Tom? Isn't Black Bob after you as well, Payton?'

'Damn you…' Tupper swore. He clutched the knife tighter, but as he stepped forward, Tom Norris stood shakily in his way.

'If he doesn't kill you, the law will. They'll hang you – hang you all,' Mary screamed.

'I don't want to hang, Tom,' Payton shouted. He winced at the thought and cowered back. 'I didn't kill Jankes. It wasn't me that did him. They'll believe me if I tell them, won't they?'

Slowly, hesitantly, fearfully, Tom's hand slipped

inside his pocket and came out with a knife. Tupper glowered a black look at him.

'You be careful, lad, if you wants to do that,' he said quietly. 'And if you're thinking of ratting on me, Payton, I'll find you, make no mistakes about that.'

'Come on, you two, wake up before it's too late,' Mary shouted. 'There's two of you, and two of us, and only one of him. Take Milverton's offer – it's better than the hangman's.'

Payton edged away towards the door and Davey Tupper scowled.

'If you try to run, Payton,' he snarled and flashed the knife at him as a warning. He turned towards Mary. 'You poison-mouthed little vixen. I'll shut it once and for all.'

The thief's mouth was tight and compressed. Without a moment's further pause, not once turning his head left or right, looking straight at her with a savage resolution, he rushed forward, the knife held high in his hand. He tried to slip past Tom and the two collided, falling across the table and sprawling, spitting and snarling, on to the floor. The oil lamp fell and shattered and fire ran quickly along the ancient floorboards, kindled by the dried paper littering the planks. Both men sprang up. Knives drawn and crouching low, they began to circle each other slowly in the growing smoke.

'I ain't mixing with cold murder – she's a girl,' Tom

said, his frightened eyes held firm on Tupper's knife as it danced from side to side.

'You yellow bilge rat. I knew I'd have to deal with you sooner or later. Make your peace with the devil when you see him.'

With that, Tupper rushed forward. The two men feigned thrusts with the knives, stepping forward, drawing back, the blades flashing and slashing, curving through the air. Each man dodged as the knives weaved around and about.

Mary and Archie edged towards the hole in the floor, but the flames were blocking their way. The fire had taken hold and was running along to the opening and up the walls, cracking and spitting at them.

'When I'm done here, you're next, Payton,' Tupper shouted.

'Murder! Murder!' Payton cried, running towards the door. Almost tripping over his feet, he clawed it open and started down the hallway.

Almost immediately, there came a hideous scream from the passage that froze everyone's limbs to marble. Payton Norris flew back through the door, clutching his stomach. He lifted his bloody hands to his face, gazed unbelievingly at them, and then slowly sank to the floor. His eyes bulged, his ashen face was stricken with pain, his lips trembled in a fearful prayer.

At that moment, a dark figure rushed in towards Tom

Norris. Tom gasped in utter amazement. Blood was spreading an ugly red blossom across his white shirt. He dropped his knife and fell on to his knees.

The thief, Tupper, gasped in horror as the dark figure turned towards him. A hideous grin creased the scar on the dirty face. The left eye narrowed, but the right one, crimson red, was wide open and glimmered brightly. He pointed a knife towards the thief.

'Mr Boots sends his regards,' Black Bob said. With an animal cry, he flew forward. The two men tumbled across the floor.

Mary froze in shock. She could not take her eyes off Tom Norris, who, kneeling, began to slump forward, clutching his stomach. Flames sprang up around him; he seemed to be burning in hell. Mary stumbled awkwardly towards him, as if her body was no longer hers to command. Her breath rasped as the smoke engulfed them. Her heart shuddered in her chest and seemed to stop.

'Come on,' Archie screamed. 'We've got to go.'

He grabbed Mary and began to pull her away. She fought his hand and stumbled forward as the burning wood crackled and snapped around them.

'We've got to help… him…' she stuttered.

Tom Norris looked at her directly, perplexed, disbelieving, pleading, as if begging for help. His face was drained of colour as the flames licked around him and the smoke engulfed him.

'Ain't nothing we can do,' Archie said.

'Archie, I can't–'

'We can't help him. He's dead!'

The words were like a blow from a hammer. *He's dead, he's dead, he's dead* echoed in her mind. She tried to drag her vision away. Vaguely remembering a purpose, she reached her hand out mechanically, feeling as if it belonged to someone else. She snatched the bundle of letters just as Archie grabbed her, dragging her, jostling her and pushing her through the smoke and the flames. Together, they dropped through the hole in the floor as a horrific scream erupted from within the house.

The icy black waters of the Thames closed around her head, muffling her hearing and entering her mouth and nose. Mary clawed her way upwards as the undertow gripped her. Spluttering and coughing, her arms flailing, she broke the surface and gasped in the cold river air. The currents swirled around her. The shock of the frigid water brought her to her senses and she remembered who she was.

'Archie! Archie!' Mary screamed. Her eyes burned. She saw the lights on the quayside and struck out towards them. Clawing against the currents, she struggled, fighting for breath and spitting the sour water from her mouth. She could feel all her strength draining away, siphoned off by the icy river. Her aching arms flailed feebly. She was sinking. Dragged down by her wet dress, she closed her eyes.

To her utter relief, she felt someone grabbing her, pulling her up, rescuing her, spinning her around.

'Archie!' Mary screamed when she broke the surface. She gulped in the air, turned around and saw the blood-red eye of Black Bob inches away. Behind her, the blazing building illuminated his wild grizzled face. He had hold of her arm and was prising the letters out of her hand.

'Give them to me,' he spat. 'Give them to me, damn you.'

Mary screamed. She felt his fingers on the top of her head, pressing her down. Then she was underwater again. He held her firmly as he clutched the hand with the letters. Mary kicked hard against his grip. The dirty water rushed up her nose. She reached up as high as she could.

There came two loud bangs. His grip loosened and released and Mary felt herself sinking. She was falling, further and further down, the river taking her to the sea.

When she opened her eyes, she saw Black Bob's face. His single red eye was looking at her. A bloody hand was holding a bloody knife. A smile broke his scarred face. His visage shimmered and wavered as if washed away by the current, and morphed and changed into the anguished face of Tom Norris.

Mary reached out to grab him, but he was moving away. 'Come,' he was saying with a silent voice. 'Do not be afraid.' She closed her eyes as she sank. Deep and deeper she fell, into the icy, murky, silent waters. Dark and darker it became. She held her breath. Her lungs were bursting. She was drifting further and further down, gasping one last prayer for mercy.

'Come with me,' Tom whispered, 'come with me to the sea.'

27

ON THE QUAYSIDE IN LIMEHOUSE

A strong hand was pulling her, dragging her up. Someone had hold of her arm. The grip was firm and unyielding. She broke the surface, the walls of the quay scraping her shins and elbows. Her hands touched solid ground.

She lay on the cobblestones, gasping and panting, coughing and spluttering, revelling in the pain that said she was alive. The foul waters burning her eyes.

'Calm yourself, calm yourself,' a deep voice said, 'you're safe now.'

An elderly white-bearded face was bending over her. The face was as wet as hers, and smiling. The keen eyes were kind and the voice soothing and comfortingly reassuring. For a moment, Mary wondered if she was dead after all.

'Mary! Mary!' Archie shouted and rushed up to her.

'Aye, lad, she's safe,' the bearded man said. 'Try some deep breaths, miss. Cough some of that water out of your lungs.'

Archie fell on his knees and hugged Mary tightly. She started to cry. Her body heaved and shuddered as she coughed. She spat the drool from deep inside her throat and clung tightly to Archie.

A crowd had gathered. She watched the faces on the quayside, caught in the light of the blazing building, fearful that one might be Black Bob or Davey Tupper. A line had formed from the water's edge to the fire. Buckets were being passed along it, but the fire had taken hold. The building burned like a beacon.

Then, through weary, aching eyes, Mary made out three bodies by the quayside. She felt a sickness bubble inside her stomach when she recognised Payton Norris, his brother Tom and the thief, Davey Tupper. Someone must have dragged them from their funeral pyre. They lay slumped on the frosty ground, as cold as the night.

Uncontrollable shivers wracked her body. Someone placed a blanket around her shoulders. Mary drew it tight, Archie supporting her. He held her firmly as she watched the dead.

The elderly white-bearded gentleman was standing away from the crowd. In one hand, he clutched a revolver, and at his feet lay the fearful figure of Black Bob. In the light of the flickering flames, Mary saw that the assassin still clutched his bloody knife in his frozen lifeless hand. His face was hideously contorted, made more so by the livid scar. His left eye was closed, but his right eye, crimson and bright, gazed glimmering and blind into the night sky.

Inspector Lestrade was running up towards the gentleman. Some way away, Mary could hear the clanging bells of a fire engine.

It was a struggle to get to her feet, and when she did, Mary went to sit wearily upon a doorstep. She was bewildered. Her thoughts were lost and swirled around inside her mind. But she could not help thinking all of this was her fault. The feeling of guilt twisted her stomach sharply and the sickness seemed to well into her throat. She had been the one who wanted to find Davey Tupper. She knew it was dangerous; she should have sought help from those who were knowledgeable in such work. Then maybe things would have worked out better. She had nearly died, and unforgivably, she had almost got Archie killed as well.

And now he was speaking to her.

She could not make out his words. She saw his lips moving, but no sound came from them. Her eyes wandered. She saw the three bodies by the building. She saw Black Bob. She saw the hustle and bustle of people fighting the fire. The building shuddered and began to collapse, folding into itself, silently slumping into the Thames.

The man with the white beard was pointing to her as he spoke to Lestrade. Now she could hear everyone speaking, all talking at once. Everything that had happened, and was happening, seemed to play through her mind at the same moment.

Suddenly she arose. She drew her wet sleeve across her eyes, wiped away her tears and pushed Archie aside.

Turning, Mary walked away from the blazing building. Someone was calling her, but it was no more than an echo. It seemed far away and lost in the night. She quickened her pace, hurrying on. Then she was running. Faster and faster she went, charging deep into the night until she was completely exhausted.

She stopped, panting deeply, her heart thundering in her chest, her flooded mind remembering everything. Her wet clothes clung to her, dragging her downwards. She was shivering. The acrid smoke was in her nose. The taste of the dirty water was in her mouth. The tortured face of Tom Norris rose before her eyes. Mary sank onto her knees and cried.

'*He's dead*,' she heard Archie say.

'I can't help you,' she wept.

Footsteps were running behind her. Mary could hear them come closer, closer, closer still as her heavy eyes flickered and drew shut. She heard no more. It was as if the black waters of the river had risen up and swallowed her again.

28
THE GHOST OF TOM NORRIS

The fat tabby stretched himself magnificently. His paws trembled when fully extended and the claws flicked out. Then he lazily drew them back. He gazed around as if bored and settled himself again. Tucking his head down, he flicked his tail around and across his nose, and yawned. Mary brushed her fingers across the warm, soft, silky fur. The tabby nipped a finger as if to warn her – *do not disturb my sleep.* His pink tongue licking his lips, he closed his eyes and slumbered into sleep once more.

'Ah! You're awake,' the friendly voice of Dr Watson whispered.

Mary looked around with tired eyes. The doctor's face was smiling from above. He was peering at a thermometer, and then shook it vigorously.

'She'll be back to normal soon,' he said.

She was in Dot and Sossie's room, in the small girls' bed. She wanted to say something, but her throat was burning. And then she noticed him.

In the corner, Tom Norris sat patiently, looking at her. His face was pale, drained bloodless, his eyes cold and lifeless, his white shirt stained red.

'The fever has broken,' Dr Watson was saying, his voice far away. 'She'll recover by degrees now. Good healthy broth is what she needs.'

'She's in the right household for that,' Grandma Dibble's voice came from somewhere in the room.

'As I suspected. Rest as well. A week and she'll be up and about as normal.'

Mary closed her eyes.

'LEAVE HER ALONE, SOSSIE,' ARCHIE BARKED.

'I'm only tucking in the sheet,' Sossie complained.

'School! Now!' Archie said.

'O-ooh!' Sossie moaned.

'You as well, Dot.'

'It's arithmetic, Archie. I know my tables already.'

'Well, help the others who don't.'

Tom Norris was sitting quietly beside Mary. He was smiling, but his eyes were closed. He said he wanted to tell her something and leant forward to whisper it. But his voice was garbled and the words were lost.

Tom sat back and was quiet again.

'"I have had so much to do inside the house," the detective said evasively. "My colleague, Mr Lestrade, is here. I had relied upon him to look after this..."

'Oh! Awake are we?' Grandpa Dibble said and put the book down that he was reading aloud. 'One of Dr Watson's. He gave it to me to read to you. You'll be up and about in no time now, he says. Remember Ella? She came to see you. She brought you a little doll she made from cotton and thread. But that damned cat ripped it apart.'

Tom Norris was seated on Dot's bed. His eyes were half-open. He was still and silent. He seemed at peace. His body was transparent. He looked about the room, up and down and across, his face calm and restful, like he was relaxing after a long day's work, and it was the weekend, and there was nothing to do, and there was nowhere to be, and nothing to want, just his bed and his rest to look forward to.

'Grandma tried to fix it, but it's beyond repair.'

'OSCAR! WHAT ARE YOU DOING HERE?' MARY SAID – for a moment, she'd thought she was back in her little attic room at the Grimwigs'. She grabbed the cat, pulling him up the bed, but he dug his claws in, dragging the blanket along with him. He gazed up mournfully, as if any disturbance to his sleep was a cause for grief.

Archie was carrying a bowl of broth and sat down beside the bed. The cat lifted his head, sniffing at the bowl.

'Fat, lazy good-for-nothing…You've been fed, so get your snout away. This ain't for you.'

Mary managed to sit up, panting a little with the effort. Then she ate greedily. Archie had brought some bread and Mary used it to mop up the remaining broth. Only when she finished did she glance around nervously, her eyes quick and furtive. It was not lost on Archie.

'What's wrong?' he asked.

Mary gave a sheepish smile and shook her head. Tom Norris was no more than a transparent sheen. He looked satisfied, as if his vigil had come to an end and he could finally go to his rest.

'How long have I been here?' she asked.

'The best part of a week. It's Sunday. You've been in and out of it. Dr Watson's been over, making sure you're all right.'

'Did I faint?'

'You drank the Thames – stupid thing to do. I had the

good sense to keep my trap shut. Rest up a bit and I'll tell you more later.'

Mary slid back down, drawing the blanket closer. The cat troubled himself to become comfortable again. Mary glanced around the room – Tom Norris was no longer there.

ARCHIE, GRANDPA AND GRANDMA DIBBLE SAT BESIDE her bed. Opposite sat Dot and Sossie.

'How did Oscar get here?' Mary asked as she stroked the cat, who for once was awake.

'Emma brought him here in a shopping basket,' Archie said. 'Seems as if Mr Grimwig's packed up and let all his staff go – fired the lot of them.' Mary looked up in concern. 'All except Mr Boots, apparently.'

'Poor Emma,' Mary said.

'Not so poor. She's found a position in Mayfair,' said Archie. 'With the Earl of Marshmere.'

'I don't understand,' Mary said.

'He appreciated her honesty, apparently, and gave her a position as a parlour maid – I think Mr Holmes had something to do with it.'

'Oh! That is nice of him. What about me and the Grimwigs and the police?' Mary looked worried. 'What happened to the letters? I had hold of them when we jumped, Archie. Did I let them go?'

Archie nodded to the table next to the bed. A mass of crumpled, crinkled brown-black-stained paper lay there. Most of the pages were stuck together, and where they were loose, the ink had run until the words were indecipherable. Just the printed headers were visible to indicate they were from the Earl of Marshmere. But whatever message they contained, words of love or otherwise, had been lost forever when they came into contact with the dirty waters of the Thames.

'You held on to them for dear life,' Archie said. 'You were still holding them when we got you home.'

'But they're gone.' Mary was despondent. 'Now how am I going to clear my name?'

Dr Watson stepped back into the room, wiping his hands on a towel. He slipped an arm through his coat sleeve, ready to leave.

'So, how's my patient?' he asked.

'How can I thank you, Dr Watson?' Mary said.

'There is no charge, Mary. Why, it's been my pleasure to treat *Bare-knuckles Jessie* for a second time.'

Mary smiled, remembering when she'd first heard that title.

'Mr Holmes asked me to convey his best wishes, Mary,' Dr Watson said. 'You did well, he bid me say. Not as well as some, but better than most, were his words – which you may take as high praise. You will make a detective yet, he declared. You should have come to *him*; the matter was dire and dangerous. But you did well, of that he was adamant. He has spoken to Lestrade and explained the circumstances as far as he knows them – which I suspect is most, if not all of the pertinent facts – and your name shall be cleared.'

'But how did he know?'

'Archie told him the tale. The rest he conjectured. I was sorry I missed it, I'm sure it was a good story. You need fear the Grimwigs no more. While they may not face the full force of the law – there is not sufficient evidence of their wrongdoings and the Earl will not compromise himself to provide any – James Grimwig will, nevertheless, find his hands tied every which way he cares to move. I have been told the Earl is a vengeful man, and now that there are no more restraints, he is free to exact his retribution. The Grimwigs' elevation to the peerage is where the Earl's first blow fell. Shortly you may read how the mighty have tumbled. London has become too small a place for them; they have closed the house in Regent's Park and have relocated to Manchester.'

'And what of the Earl?'

'Ah! Well, what can one say? The door there is shut tight and we can but speculate. If there is a scandal, Mr Holmes suspects it will never see the light of day – her

Ladyship will see to that and no doubt she will deal with her husband in her own way. Holmes said that you were right about Mr Jankes, too. Archie mentioned his part in your little escapade. So, my very best, Mary Finch. I shall look forward to seeing you up and about in the near future.'

Dr Watson stopped and turned back.

'Oh! I almost forgot. Mr Holmes did an enquiry. He wondered if you could speculate as to its meaning. Mr Boots, the butler, owns a house overlooking Barnes Green. Odd that a butler should be so well off and yet be so employed. Holmes asked if you thought the same.'

She smiled weakly as the doctor left. *It was odd*, she thought.

'Here,' Archie said and handed Mary a newspaper of a few days ago.

MYSTERIOUS DEATHS IN LIMEHOUSE

The identities of the men found so cruelly murdered and outraged at Limehouse yesterday morning have at last been decided, and henceforth, they are to be known as David Arthur Tupper, of Whitechapel, Thomas Norris and his brother Payton, itinerants of no fixed abode, and Robert Johnson (known as Black Bob) also of no fixed abode. Except for Robert Johnson, it cannot be said, with any degree of certainty, what the reasons were for their deaths, but a falling out of thieves is suspected.

By a chance of fate, the mother of David Tupper, a Mrs Virginia Tupper, was found murdered on the last Sunday in Hanbury Street, Whitechapel. Police are not linking the crimes.

Captain George Turner, of the Steam Ship Arcturus, who shot dead Mr Robert Johnson on the occasion of his assault on a young girl, will not be charged, according to Inspector Lestrade of Scotland Yard. His praiseworthy action…

'BUT OUR NAMES?' MARY ASKED ARCHIE.

'Mr Holmes saw to it that we were not mentioned.'

Beneath the report, sandwiched between a story about a gas explosion in Kilburn and a scandal in a law firm, Mary made out another story:

The Body of Dorian Jankes was pulled from the Thames east of Blackwall Reach.

She placed the paper down and gazed into space. For all the hardship that Davey Tupper had caused her, she felt sorry for him. Katie Tupper was right – he was a pickpocket and should have stuck to what he knew best.

'Isn't it funny,' Mary said. 'We owe our lives to Black Bob. If he hadn't been following us…

'I've been thinking, Archie. Mr Grimwig was playing

for time. That's why he didn't have me arrested that day. I'm willing to believe that he wasn't trying to run me down, either; I think he wanted to scare me so I would lead him to Davey. He knew they'd be blackmailing him and had to act quickly. The longer he waited, the harder it would be for him to fix it. He had to hurry before they settled.

'So, I had to be dismissed. If he'd kept me on after the robbery, then I'd be in the house and wouldn't have led him to the letters. He had Black Bob and Mr Boots follow me. And I led Bob straight to Mrs Tupper, and then to Katie – despite my disguise.

'But by the time we went to Limehouse, it didn't matter to Mr Grimwig if he got the letters back or not, just as long as the Earl didn't get them. Even if they were destroyed, he could continue blackmailing after a sort–'

'By pretending he still had them?'

Mary nodded. 'And of course, he didn't reckon on Milverton. He couldn't risk him getting the letters – Milverton would have destroyed him.'

'And Jankes?'

'Inspector Lestrade called him an opportunist, remember? I guess he wanted a share of the blackmail also. Somehow he must have found out about it. It was him that got Davey to double-cross Milverton.'

'Well, the letters are all gone and the Earl knows

about it, and now he's set on doing the destroying,' Archie said.

'I was stupid, Archie. I should have seen Mr Holmes – he knows more about these things than I do. Because of that, I nearly got you killed. I'm so sorry. I just thought I could solve it by myself. I should have known better.'

'Well, Mr Holmes seems to think you did all right. And I'm grateful for your quick thinking: going on about working for Milverton and all that – that was genius. If anything, you saved us, not Black Bob. And we ain't dead.'

'But Davey is. And Payton and Tom… and Jankes and Mrs Tupper–'

'None of which is your fault – just you remember that. Tell me, did you figure all that stuff out before they caught us?'

Mary gave a shy smile. 'It was the only thing that made any sense to me.'

'But you knew about the letters?'

The smile left her lips as the memories came back. 'I guessed. Something small enough to be in the jewel bag. Different enough so she'd know it wasn't there – that's why she said *"Where are they?"* straight away. Then Milverton – a blackmailer – and what Katie said about getting rich quick. The Earl clinched it when I found out that he was a commoner, and Emma telling me about his argument with Mr G.'

'Something worth more than money!' Archie smiled. 'I just wished you'd told me, and then I would have played along. Of course, I would have figured it out myself.' He winked. 'Except I ain't read all those books you have. But I'll tell you what I did figure out: Boots and Mr Grimwig were partners.'

He nodded proudly. Mary smiled and Archie sighed. 'Oh! I see.'

'I think that's what Mr Holmes meant about Boots's house in Barnes Green.'

'Mary, did you know that Archie's been up to see Mr Holmes?' Sossie said.

'He went inside his flat, he did,' Dot said.

'Spoke to him, he did.'

They both looked at their brother with pride.

'Yeah, well, me and him had some words,' Archie said self-importantly. He looked over at Mary and saw her eyes had dropped. 'Come on, you two. You can stay up late tonight.'

'Can we play in your room, Archie?' Dot asked and they ran off before he could answer.

Archie walked to the door. Then he stopped and turned.

'He's gone. You know that, don't you? Tom Norris. He's gone. He ain't back there, nor over there, neither, nor sitting on the bed, nor standing in the corner.' Mary looked puzzled. 'Nah! I don't see him – just you, when you were feverish and shouting. He's gone, Mary, and ain't coming back.'

Mary closed her eyes. She was tired. She could remember seeing in Tom's eyes the knowledge that he was dying, his trembling hands. She'd wanted to help. But she couldn't. No matter what she'd done, she couldn't have helped him. Was that what he'd tried to whisper to her? Was it thanks for thinking about helping him? Or to say that she couldn't, and it wasn't her fault? In the end, he'd tried to protect her and Archie. Did that mean he had saved his soul?

'I hope so, Archie,' Mary said.

29

TO MRS JANE ROSE GRADY OF HOLLAND PARK

Mary knew of Mrs Jane Rose Grady. Her house, a large redbrick detached property that rambled over several floors, bordered Holland Park. She was a redheaded Irishwoman of more than sixty years. Patrick Grady was her husband. There were rumours that he'd made his money as a Plantation owner in Virginia and smuggling anything from rum to slaves. He went down when his ship, the *Jane Rose*, struck rocks in the Delaware Bay in a storm in 1860, and since then, for over thirty years, Mrs Grady had lived alone, devoting herself to charity and the betterment of her sex.

Mary stood at the grand entranceway of Mrs Grady's house. Beside her were Dot, Sossie and Archie. She held Ella's hand.

'Is this the place, Mary?' Ella asked in amazement.

Never before had she been inside a house as lavish as this. And now she was about to do just that.

'Grand, ain't it?' Mary said.

'It's a palace,' Sossie said.

'It's here I'm going to work?' Ella asked in disbelief.

'Well, after a fashion,' Mary nodded.

'Not selling matches with Granny?'

'No. The lady of the house has a proposition for you. And you'll be in the warm, with a room of your own. Your granny and mum can visit anytime they like. And she'll pay you – after a fashion,' Mary winked.

Dot and Sossie looked at each other with open mouths as Mary rang the bell.

'She won't have to go to school,' Sossie whispered to Dot, who nodded.

A rather grand silver-haired butler, dressed in sober black and wearing white Egyptian cotton gloves, answered the bell. He carried an air of indifference and escorted them to an extremely large and bright drawing room, where they sat gingerly on Chesterfield sofas and waited.

'Madam apologises for the delay. She will be here soon,' he said without looking at anyone in particular, as if speaking to the room.

As they waited, a silent maid, a young girl from the West Indies, served tea. Over the fireplace, a very pretty, elegant lady, no more than her early twenties, looked down at them. She smiled radiantly with ruby-red lips. Her eyes twinkled. Locks of red hair framed her round face. A red rose was balanced on her fingers. She was surrounded by a mixture of portrait and landscape and still-life paintings and framed photographs that hung on rich flock wallpaper. But such was her presence that she dominated the room and everyone felt compelled to talk in whispers.

Ten minutes passed, and then the painting came to life. Many years older, but unmistakably the same woman, Jane Grady entered the room. She spoke to them for half an hour about nothing in particular, as if they were friends who had last met only yesterday. An easy companion, she was funny and pleasant.

Then after speaking privately to Mary and Ella, she stood up and said, 'Come, Mary, walk with me.'

They passed through a French window and stood on a small terrace, overlooking a discreet formal garden, where the lady told Mary about her life. She spoke briefly, not dwelling on details.

'My regret has always been not having children,' she concluded. 'Patrick wanted children, too, but alas, that was not to be so. Fate had other plans for him and me. Now, do you think my intentions wrong?'

'Adopting Ella? No, Mrs Grady. My only concern – well, it's this. I missed my parents so much when I went into service. But it was different with me. My parents were dead and I had no living relatives, except a brother, and I don't know what happened to him.' Mary fiddled with the half locket she wore. 'But Ella has a granny and a mum. What about them? She loves them and will miss them, that I know.'

'I intend to look after them as well. There can be no other course. I will make sufficient arrangements. I want Ella to be happy, otherwise what is the point? Other than to satisfy an old lady's vanity.'

'I don't get it. I mean, Grandma Dibble. How does she know people like you and the others?'

'Ah! Now there's a story. There's lots you do not know about that old woman.' Mrs Grady smiled. 'Now, tell me, will you accept the position of maid? I can use a bright girl like you. Someone who can think on her feet and is brave and willing to take chances. A resourceful, clever girl, with some brains. It is an unfair world, and a harsh one for a child like you, Mary, orphaned and penniless. If the truth were known, it's just as harsh for an old lady like me, childless and alone. My best years are behind me. Yours are in front. We can help each other. You see, Mary, everyone's suffering is the same; it's just our devils that are different. So, what say you?'

'I need a job, and I could really like this one,' Mary said. 'But I've got plans to better myself, Mrs Grady.'

'Good, because I would have it no other way. It is done. Now, tell me about him.' With that, Mrs Grady reached out to the locket around Mary's neck. 'Is this he, your brother?'

The face of a small boy occupied the broken half of the locket. Mary nodded. She told Mrs Grady what she remembered about her brother, about the accident that had claimed her parents' lives and her desire to be reunited with him again.

'I want to find him,' Mary ended. 'I will look for him when I can.'

'Then we *can* help each other, can we not?' Mrs Grady said.

They went back inside. The small girls, now at ease, were talking freely. For a while, Mrs Grady listened. She seemed lost in the sounds of their voices.

'Cor!' Sossie said. 'You're lucky, Ella. You've got a job and don't have to go to school!'

'Yeah. No school,' Dot said enviously. 'I wish I was living here.'

Ella smiled rather proudly.

'No school,' and both sisters sighed together.

'School,' said Mrs Grady loudly, and the girls stiffened at the mention of the word, 'is a place Ella will certainly go. Four hours a day, five days a week, fifty-two weeks a year, until she becomes a lady, no more and no less. She will be allowed Christmas Day and Good Friday off – St Patrick's day if I am satisfied.'

Sossie and Dot's mouths gaped in horror at the appalling prospect. Ella swallowed loudly.

'Education, Misses Dibbles, is a woman's emancipation. It is our freedom. It makes us equal to any man, anywhere, at any time. In due course, Ella Sutton will make a splendid addition to the Women's Suffrage Committee. She may run it. Who knows, with sufficient education, we may even have a woman as Prime Minister one day.'

'Hah!' Archie said, surprised at both his boldness and how loud his one-word opinion sounded in the very large room.

'Hah indeed!' Mrs Grady replied and looked the boy up and down with a probing eye that seemed to strip him bare. 'We can be sure of one thing, young man: even in our most desperate hour, *you* will never be called upon to fulfil that fine honour.'

With the arrangements made, Mary and her companions walked slowly and quietly back towards Baker Street. Mary would be employed as a maid. Mrs Grady would be Ella's guardian. Oscar would take up duties as the house cat – though Mrs Grady did not know that yet. And Dot and Sossie would still attend school, much to their irritation.

Mary was so lost in thought that she almost did not notice the familiar carriage that drew up across the road. The plump-faced man, a frozen smile on his lips, his grey eyes bright, tipped his hat to her. When she realised who it was, her heart sank. She hesitated, and then started across the road. Archie reached out to stop her, but Mary walked past him.

'I see you are better despite your ordeal,' Mr Milverton said pleasantly.

'No thanks to you.'

'I also hear you have found employment,' and he nodded to Mrs Grady's house. Mary ignored his enquiring eyes and the meaning behind his unspoken question, and how he knew she had found a job.

'It doesn't worry you, does it?' she said, and he looked at her impassively. 'Davey Tupper and his mother are dead because of you, and his widow and child will probably end up in the workhouse. None of it worries you, does it, Mr Milverton? All the death that surrounds you really doesn't bother you. It's just about the money you can make at the expense of other people's misery.'

'Ah! I see,' and he nodded his head solemnly. 'And conscience is such a luxury, especially for one with a limited income, Miss Finch.' He smiled. 'Well, it is your choice, of course, just as it was Davey Tupper's choice. I kept my part of the bargain, he chose otherwise. Had he not done so, things would have been different. It was *he* who decided to enter a game for which he was not suited – a game amateurs should keep away from, Miss Finch. Though, I suppose I should thank you, or Davey perhaps, for removing Mr Jankes from the game. As for Mr Tupper's widow – she has status, I believe. She owns a property. Mr Tupper's mother had no other relatives; the house in Hanbury Street is now hers. And when you cast blame, do not forget the part the Grimwigs had in our little play.' He looked to the Grady residence somewhat longingly, and then back to Mary. 'Pity,' he said, smiling. 'Pity.'

Milverton raised his cane to touch the brim of his hat. Nodding slightly to say goodbye, he tapped the roof of his carriage.

Mary crossed the road back to her companions.

'What did he want?' Archie asked.

'Nothing at all,' Mary said.

'Can't we get jobs?' Dot said.

'Yeah, Dot and me could become maids as well, just like you, Mary,' Sossie said.

'And miss school?' Archie asked.

Both girls were discreetly quiet.

'And miss scoffing Grandma's pies for supper?' Mary asked.

'Oh!' Sossie said.

'Well, maybe we could come home at night,' Dot said thoughtfully.

'Yeah, we could come home at night,' Sossie agreed.

A few white flakes drifted down. By the time they reached Baker Street, it would be snowing again.

AUTHOR'S NOTES

Scullery maids were the lowest-ranked and often the youngest of the female domestic servants. They could be as young as ten years old. Duties included providing hot water for the scullery and kitchen as well as a host of other tasks: keeping the scullery clean, clearing away meat and vegetable waste, scrubbing work tables, swilling the floors, lighting the fires on the kitchen stoves. The scullery maid would perform many of these tasks in the morning before the cook came down to the kitchen.

The nineteenth century, in the United Kingdom, saw the birth of the Penny Dreadfuls (sometimes called the Penny Horrible, or Penny Awful, or Penny Blood) the type of magazine Mary is so fond of reading. These were cheap popular serial literature, each costing a penny, that have been called 'Britain's first taste of mass-produced popular culture for the young,'("Penny Dreadfuls: the Victorian equivalent of video games". *The Guardian*). The subject matters of the stories often focused on the exploits of detectives, criminals or the supernatural. In many ways, you may consider them the comics of the day.

Jack the Ripper terrorised London in 1888. The murders of at least five women have been attributed to him in or near Whitechapel, a district in London's East End. Several other murders occurring at that same period have been investigated as the work of 'Leather Apron', another of the names he was known as. The nickname Jack the Ripper originated from letters allegedly sent by the killer to Scotland Yard, the police force investigating the murders. The letters taunted officers about his crimes and they may well have been hoaxes. The Ripper was never apprehended and remains one of England's most gruesome and infamous murderers.

Charles Augustus Milverton and Inspector Lestrade (as well as Sherlock Holmes and Dr Watson) are characters taken from the writings of Sir Arthur Conan Doyle, author of the *Sherlock Holmes* stories. Some of these characters will reappear in subsequent Mary Finch adventures. You may care to read *The Adventure of*

Charles Augustus Milverton, a short story by Conan Doyle, if you wish to find out the gentleman's fate.

Lastly – old money. The currency used in this book is pounds, shillings and pence. Two farthings made a ha'penny (that is half a penny); two ha'penny made a penny; three pennies made a thruppence (a three-penny bit); two thruppence made a sixpence (sometimes called a tanner); two sixpence made a shilling (also known as a bob); two shillings made a florin; a florin and a sixpence made a half-crown; twenty shillings (or two hundred and forty pence) made a pound (a pound coin on its own was a sovereign); and twenty-one shillings made a guinea. In 1971 the United Kingdom changed to a decimal system of money, so ending a currency that was introduced in 1066 with the Norman Conquest.

ACKNOWLEDGMENTS

Thank you to all who have contributed to the writing of this book. While I would like to mention everyone may I just single out these few? Tom Conaghan who read the original manuscript and offered fantastic advice. Clay Kelly for her support. The members of the Forest Writers who patiently listened to the reading of some of the chapters, and especially to Alison Jack, who made me look good.

AFTERWORD

REVIEW REQUEST

If you have enjoyed reading this book, please leave a review on Amazon.
I read every single review and they help new readers discover my books.

For more information you can visit my website:
https://saywackwrites.com

or contact me by email:
saywackwrites@gmail.com

or come and say Hi! on my facebook page:
https://www.facebook.com/S-S-Saywack-Writes-101805885237022

ALSO BY S S SAYWACK

Mary Finch and the Thief is the first book in a series.

Follow Mary's adventure in Mary Finch and the Grey Lady, and

Mary Finch and the Spy.

To be released soon.

Printed in Great Britain
by Amazon

59517572R00149